The Flagellants

△

Other Volumes in the Black Women Writers Series

Carlene Hatcher Polite

The Flagellants

With an introduction by Claudia Tate

Beacon Press Boston

Beacon Press
25 Beacon Street
Boston, Massachusetts 02108

Beacon Press books
are published under the auspices of
the Unitarian Universalist Association of Congregations.

94 93 92 91 90 89 88 87   8 7 6 5 4 3 2 1

Library of Congress Cataloging-in-Publication Data

Polite, Carlene Hatcher.
  The flagellants.

  (Black women writers series)
  I. Title. II. Series.
PS3566.047F54   1987   83'.54   86-47874
ISBN 0-8070-6321-5 (pbk.)

To the unborn beast

introduction   Claudia Tate

Δ

When the American edition of Carlene Hatcher
Polite's *The Flagellants* appeared in 1967, critics
included it among several acclaimed novels by black
authors that had recently appeared.[1] Encouraged by
the famous French editor Dominique de Roux, Polite
finished the novel in nine months. It was written in
English, translated into French, and published in
1966 by a new French company—Christian
Bourgois—as its first title. In 1967, Farrar, Straus and
Giroux published the American edition, which had a
very successful run in cloth before Dell reissued it in
paperback. In 1975 Polite published her second novel,
Sister X and the Victims of Foul Play, a satirical
account of black people living in Europe during the
1960s. Like *The Flagellants*, this novel evolves largely
as counterpoint dialogue rather than as a series of
dramatized incidents. However, *Sister X* does not have
the technical or thematic power of Polite's first novel.

The Flagellants was a part of the surge of Afro-
American literary activity that took place during the
late sixties and early seventies, reminiscent of the
New Negro Renaissance of the 1920s and 1930s.
This impressive spate of novels included Margaret
Walker's *Jubilee* (1966), Kristin Hunter's *The Land-
lord* (1966), John A. Williams's *The Man Who Cried
I Am* (1967), Ishmael Reed's *The Free Lance Pall
Bearers* (1967), Maya Angelou's *I Know Why the*

Caged Bird Sings (1970), William Melvin Kelly's *Dem* (1967), Cecil Brown's *The Life and Loves of Mr. Jiveass Nigger* (1970), and Toni Morrison's *The Bluest Eye* (1970). Although many critics were dazzled by the daring experimentation of some of these writers, others were clearly bewildered by their playful, self-conscious texts. Polite's reviewers fell into both categories: they were either intrigued or confused by her refusal to rely on the stylistic conventions of narrative fiction with which they were familiar.

Frederic Raphael in *The New York Times Book Review*, for example labeled *The Flagellants* a "dialectical diatribe."[2] Evidently, Polite's dialogic technique of shaping her story disoriented him to the degree that he mistook Greenwich Village for "the American Black Ghetto," which he claimed was the novel's setting. Unfortunately, he projected his confusion onto his reading of the text, declaring that "Miss Polite's narrative creaks with the stresses of literary uncertainty . . . a smoke screen of words billows in the reader's eyes—until, stung, he may fail to appreciate the fire that lies behind it" (p. 40). Finally, he concluded that Polite's problem was her inability to determine to whom she was speaking. If she was speaking to him, he didn't get the message.

Another reviewer, William Hill in *Best Sellers*, conceded that Polite "has talent; but the good and the bad in her writing are so thoroughly mixed that she obviously needs guidance."[3] He also questioned the universality of her central theme:

She would be wise, too, to choose better
themes than the one in this novel. It is true that
women sometimes fasten their affections on most
unworthy objects and they are sometimes
chained by their senses, and an affair of this sort
is intensely and terribly real to the participants
and perhaps to some fellow-sufferers; but it can
be a crashing bore to the rest of the world.
(p. 140)

This comment is reminiscent of Louis Simpson's infamous remark about the absence of universal themes in Gwendolyn Brook's *Selected Poems* (1960).[4] For Simpson, the experience of American Negroes lacked universal implications, and for Hill, women's affairs of the heart were boring "to the rest of the world." Both remarks serve to remind us how instrumental the black power movement and the women's movement have been and continue to be in making us question and ultimately refute racist and sexist assumptions that black people and women of all races are inferior to white males.

A more sensitive reader, Stanley Kauffmann of *The New Republic*, was convinced that *The Flagellants* was "a marker of a new period in Negro fiction." What were troublesome stylistic elements for others were for him clear signs that Negro fiction was evolving beyond realism. Although Kauffmann's review is marked (if not marred) by his efforts to categorize Negro writing and interpret Polite's "Negritude," he did not miss her central concerns—that "Negroes must face their own psyches, molded by the

American past and the white-washed American present" and that "they have been liberated to their own species of 20th-century alienation." He concluded his review emphatically, insisting that *The Flagellants* "is a stunning accomplishment" and that it is "art and not argument."[5]

Black publications such as *Ebony, Crisis,* and *Freedomways* mentioned *The Flagellants* in listings of new books by black writers and generally cited it as an important first novel. *Negro Digest*, however, ran a review of the novel by Nikki Giovanni, in which she praised the story's naked truth: "every black woman has had her Jimson, [and has wanted] to see if he was treated with the proper respect due a black, uncastrated man."[6] Giovanni had no problem determining to whom the novel spoke. According to her, it spoke to the reality of black peoples' lives, especially to the reality of black women's lives.

The Flagellants' unusual publication history also speaks to its complex relationship with its audience and the consequences of its refusal to be bound by the historic limits of so-called Negro fiction, which demanded social realism, petitions for racial equality, and positive black character portrayals. That the novel was written in France and translated from English into French for its first printing certainly signals a break from these thematic and stylistic prescriptions, and indicates as well some unreadiness on the part of a general American audience.

French writers like Sartre, Camus, Gide, Malraux, and de Beauvoir probably had some influence on

Polite's novel inasmuch as they had a tremendous effect on all Western postmodern literature. Their stories about chilling affirmations of freedom and personal responsibility, placed in stark settings characterized by acute urban alienation, describe the human condition irrespective of race, nationality, or gender. Their texts are extremely self-conscious; they employ meditative discourse and minimal story and character development in order to probe paradoxes that qualify the lives of contemporary men and women. These writers were also among the vanguard of those who sought to create "new" literary texts that would discourage, even forbid, passive reading and easy moralizing. Such novels compel the reader to participate actively in creating textual meaning, as do plays in which the audience finds itself unwittingly interpreting the roles of the actors on stage. For these novels, the story and its meaning are the product of both the words printed on the page and the reader's active response to the process of reading them.

The Flagellants is certainly not a text that can be read passively. In fact, repeated references to the game of flagellation in the story, the novel's verbal playfulness, and the density of its language of signification point to the presence of "rules of play," or a code for reading the novel. Without an awareness of these rules, the reader is likely to misread it, seeing the novel as a confusing tirade on racial bitterness and frustration, rather than as a fictive probe into questions about racial indentity, personal responsibility, free will, and self-determination.

Ideal and Jimson are the flagellants of the novel's title. Each has abandoned a spouse to form a tempestuous relationship full of both erotic desire and piercing recriminations. The polar intensity of their emotional bond virtually scourges them. The novel draws power from repeated allusions to the act of flagellation, which calls to mind two familiar but very different types of passion. One relates to religious discipline, represented by Christ's flagellation and the martyrdom of Christian saints: the other involves erotic, sadistic pleasure reminiscent of the sexual violence of de Sade. Together, both allusions create a complicated, psychological tension within Ideal. They create, as well, a tension between Ideal's efforts to understand the motives controlling her behavior and the reader's efforts to untangle the story's meaning.

Ideal and Jimson obscure the distinction between these two types of flagellation/passion, and come to associate spiritual suffering with sadomasochistic pain. Through their relationship, the novel dramatizes questions that surround these distinctive forms of suffering. The novel asks, first, whether it is possible for Ideal and Jimson to torment each other to the point that their feelings of personal inadequacy will be numbed and, second, whether the discipline of suffering has transformative power.

Like Zora Neale Hurston's *Their Eyes Were Watching God*, published in 1937, *The Flagellants* begins with a prologue that is divided into two sections. The partial, prefatory frame of *Their Eyes* reunites Janie with her best friend, Phoeby, with whom she shares her personal history; it also prepares Janie to decipher the significance of that history. The first portion of the prologue of *The Flagellants*, on the other hand, is a direct interior monologue that shows Ideal in isolation, sorting through her memories, as she smokes a cigarette and ponders her turbulent life with Jimson:

> Smoke from both my cigarette and incense
> blow blue-gray forms into the silence. The
> lighting of another cigarette has become a sort of
> ritual, a necessary preface to my every act and
> sentiment. . . . I may be mistaken for a fool. The
> laughter's volume eases down into the same tone
> as the silence. (pp. 3-4)

The fact that she is distressed but in control, alone but not depressed makes one suspect that she is undergoing a change in character. On rereading the text, one suspects that she is evolving from a dependent, subjugated object to an autonomous, courageous subject. But unlike Janie, Ideal's transformation is incomplete at the novel's conclusion. Whereas Janie achieves psychic wholeness signified by her pulling "in her horizon like a great fish-net . . . and drap[ing] it over her shoulder,"[7] Ideal can only perceive the possibility for such wholeness—an ideal self—at the novel's closure. That possible ideal self emerges at the end of the journey through her recollected past, as she resolves the conflicts in her life.

This opening monologue prepares the action for the entire novel, and grants Ideal narrative authority, even as she recalls Jimson's perspective. Although the monologue's tone of desperation, ambivalence, even hysteria suggests that Ideal's authority is tenuous, she nevertheless gains credibility from her oblique declaration that she is no fool. She is thus the novel's principal structuring agent. The novel is rendered from her vantage point, begins emphatically in her voice, and is sustained throughout in that voice.

The second, longer section of the prologue adheres more closely to traditional third-person narration, though it too is the product of Ideal's selective recollection. Like the rest of the story, this portion of the prologue also employs minimal plot development and character detail. It does, however, prepare the reader for Ideal's struggle to understand her relationship with Jimson, and it clues the reader into the allegorical significance of their names and personal histories.

The first clue comes from Ideal's great-grandmother, who puzzles over "what possessed [Ideal's] mother to give [her] such a name" but who nevertheless gives her great-granddaughter advice that is indeed "ideal." She advises Ideal to "always walk tall" and to refuse to "bow down to anything or to anyone" unless she so chooses. Her question about the suitability of the child's name alerts the reader to the connection between the old woman's wisdom and Ideal's allegorical name. As a result, the reader expects Ideal to live up to her name and to struggle for a life marked by courage, integrity, and dignity.

The old woman's advice points out the difference between the emotional and rational ways of perceiving reality. Her limited education demands that she acquire information largely through experience, that she trust feelings over observation, and that she share her experiential wisdom with her great-granddaughter through folk narratives that separate good from evil in the manner of biblical allegories.

These didactic, subtextual, anecdotal narratives resound throughout Afro-American literature. Father John in Jean Toomer's *Cane* (1923), the grandfather in Ralph Ellison's *Invisible Man* (1952), Linda's grandmother in Harriet Jacobs's *Incident in the Life of a Slave Girl* (1861), and Nanny in Hurston's *Their Eyes* (1937), for example, all try to communicate advice to grandchildren. In Afro-American texts that center on male authority, grandfatherly advice to males usually prescribes methods for achieving racially forbidden public success. In similar texts concerned with female authority, grandmotherly advice to females traditionally prescribes feminine sexual purity as the route to personal success, which is conventionally confined within the domestic sphere. In other words, elderly female forebears repeatedly warn female children to preserve what is valued in a male-dominated society—virginity—in order to exchange it for social protection at some later date. Satisfying the demands of advice such as this is difficult if not impossible in a society that has historically regarded black women as sexual prey. Significantly, *The Flagellants* breaks with the tradition of handing down advice about female sexual propriety. In this novel, instead of exhorting Ideal to remain chaste, the great-grandmother imparts general information about human nature, social interaction, and the world at large. Despite this important difference, the advice given to Ideal by her great-grandmother shares a basic communicative flaw with other such advice in the Afro-American literary tradition: because of the differences in experience between the generations, the grandchildren do not know how to interpret the folk texts of their grandparents' wisdom.

The Flagellants' prologue is full of instances in which Ideal fails to appreciate her great-grandmother's wisdom. For example, she admonishes the child not to try to outrun her shadow (p. 6). Ideal realizes the prudence of such advice, inasmuch as experience has taught her that to do so is physically impossible. However, the deeper psychological implications about futile efforts to abandon the dark side of human character, the Jungian "shadow" or the Freudian "id," are initially lost on Ideal because the old woman does not explain this aspect of human nature in terms that Ideal immediately understands. The novel's dedication—"to the unborn beast"— underscores the significance of reining in this imperfectible self, the beast that dwells within us all.

Later in the prologue, Ideal's great-grandmother explains that the devil is not simply an abstraction but "a permanent resident walking, talking, visiting freely among [them]" (p. 13). Rather than explain evil as a fundamental human trait, the great-grandmother personifies evil as the devil, seeing his presence in the tall entangling weeds in a field. This image of evil, in turn, becomes entangled in the child's mind with images of sunflowers, seeds, and maggots. Once again Ideal initially misses the essential lesson of her great-grandmother's wisdom by failing to read her anecdotal text.

In attempting to warn Ideal about the many guises of the devil, the great-grandmother also provides the allegorical clue to Jimson's name. When Ideal and her great-grandmother take a shortcut through some tall weeds, the old woman again mentions the devil:

"That's the devil trying his best to keep us from going on, child," the woman reckoned.
    The weeds whipped Ideal's legs until their color was drained. They bled little drips of blackish-red blood. (p. 13)

In making this comment the old woman marks an analogy between Jimson as the poisonous jimson-weed and the devil. An additional prefiguration appears in Ideal's dream of the weed coming to life as "a glazed green boy with an iridescent mouth laugh[ing] like a hyena" (p. 15).

Both sections of the prologue—the interior monologue and the history of Ideal's childhood—provide the code for understanding how to read the novel. The prologue invites the reader to solve the puzzle of the text, to determine why Ideal subjects herself to Jimson's game of flagellation and why she ultimately withdraws from playing the game. The answers to the puzzle lie embedded in her past life in the black community of Black Bottom.

Ideal is an attractive young black woman, a former dancer, whose childhood experiences are largely a composite of her racial history. Despite the poverty, ignorance, and oppression of her Southern past, Ideal is nevertheless imbued with the will to survive with dignity, integrity, and honor, although that legacy of survival is threatened by the Southern community's own code and punitive prescriptions for a "willful" girl. According to one woman in the community, Ideal must be controlled; she must "walk a chalked line" (p. 16). "She predicted that unless the child had the devil beaten out of her constantly, her high-strung and willful nature would be her ruination" (ibid). Strict and recurring punishment, then, initiates Ideal's masochistic tendencies. She habitually seeks to prove both her goodness and capacity to love by demonstrating her willingness to suffer: "Punishment became the cockeyed plumb line by which the depth of love could be measured and angled—a divining rod. . . . It was a sign of evil to possess the nerve to fight back, to defend one's nature" (p. 17). The physical punishment inflicted on Ideal does not beat willfulness out of her; rather, it impresses it deeply upon her consciousness as guilt. And, in order to purge that guilt, she invites increasing and life-threatening levels of suffering.

The old-time religion of Ideal's Southern heritage, which shapes her knowledge of God, also contributes to her willingness to suffer. She associates the tall, magnificent preacher who personified absolute power—"the giant's will" (p. 11)—with God. She then recognizes God's presence in her, as her religion dictates, as "suffering the weight of a bloody cross" (p. 20). Her religion teaches her that God's presence in her is reflected in her own suffering, which becomes tangible evidence of the degree of her goodness and capacity to love.

Jimson, on the other hand, does not directly experience the Southern black subservience, poverty, and historic inferiority that partly explain Ideal's psychology of victimage. Instead, he experiences the legacy of slavery indirectly through observing the behavior of Papa Boo. After serving as his former master's chauffeur for forty years, Papa Boo rents a room in Jimson's childhood home. Jimson sees Papa Boo disparagingly as the symbolic embodiment of the docile nigger, "the handkerchief head," the "Uncle Tom." Ironically, Papa Boo is not only Jimson's mythic boogie man and the white man's stereotyped projection of evil, he is also the figurative representation of Jimson's "id," his "shadow," the racial self obliterated by economic privilege and familial protectiveness.

Jimson and Papa Boo also serve one another in mutually dependent roles. On the one hand, Papa Boo projects his feelings of racial subjugation onto Jimson by casting him in the role of the bad nigger, the "black dog," and ultimately into the comprehensive figure for all evil—the Prince of Darkness. Jimson, in turn, vehemently condemns Papa Boo's hypocritical behavior and rejects him outright rather than understand Papa Boo's behavior as the product of feelings of inadequacy. Like Ideal, Jimson struggles to escape a fundamental part of himself. However, this "shadow" is not simply a dark projection of himself, but also a separate and distinct person, Papa Boo. Because Jimson perceives his shadow as separate from himself, he falsely believes that escape is possible. Unfortunately, in trying to reject both his real and symbolic shadows, he becomes entangled in what he repudiates, and ultimately he becomes infected with Papa Boo's dreaded disease of subservience.

Jimson's father has tried to protect him from that disease, vowing that "no child of [his] would ever . . . hold his hat in his hand before a living soul" (p. 69). But the father's way of mitigating the power of racism on his son's life is raising him to be a gentleman and giving him a life of economic privilege: "tennis lessons, piano lessons, horseback riding . . . his own automobile [at] fourteen—a thorough-bred pony at seven . . . clothes . . . from the finest stores" (pp. 68-69). By providing his son with "anything he thought he wanted," Jimson's father actually weakens rather than fortifies his son's emotional resistance to feelings of racial inferiority. Moreover, by attempting to make race an irrelevant factor in Jimson's life, he also denies Jimson access to the history of black people's heroic struggle to survive racial oppression with dignity.

Having been protected from this history, Jimson has an understanding of Afro-American heritage limited to his observations of Papa Boo and his exposure to sociological studies of the so-called aberrant social behavior of black Americans. As a result, Jimson relates to Ideal as sociological type rather than actual human being. He repeatedly assaults her with the popular rhetoric of race, referring to her, for example, as "the effete symbol of the enduring black matriarch" (p. 178) and "the white man's nocturnal dream" (p. 176). He similarly denigrates black men as psychically castrated, subjugated, and impotent (p. 187). The more he relies on such rhetoric, the more entangled he becomes in eloquent, circular arguments about racial stereotypes. Paradoxically, his effort to refute these arguments gives them the power to entrap him. Rather than accept the imperfectible side of his nature, Jimson traps himself not within his personal shadow—the projections of his own negative aspirations—but within Papa Boo's shadow of racial insecurity.

Ideal is initially struck by the splendor of Jimson's speech, by his aggressive manner, and by his arrogant intelligence, all of which she identifies with her childhood perception of absolute power—"the giant's will." However, when she eventually submits him to the test of her great-grandmother's wisdom, she discovers his rhetoric is a mask that conceals his feelings of inadequacy not only from others but from himself as well. This knowledge allows her to break the cycle of pain, as she further realizes her gross error: "I have become so desperate in my search for the giant that I allow myself to be fooled by beards" (p. 190). Ideal realizes that she has picked neither a flower nor a blade of grass, but a weed. More importantly, she sees that she alone must assume full responsibility for her suffering:

> It is not a floating God on high, contriving punishment, deciding who can withstand a dose or two. It is not a red-tail devil below, taking out ashes, proposing strategies to fix the foe. It is an ignorant woman named Ideal straining to produce the whole of pain, holding her breath to keep from living. (p. 192)

With the assumption of responsibility comes the possibility of freedom. Ideal lays claim to personal freedom, and comes to criticize both herself and Jimson, constructively. At this point in her development she is ready to live up to the standard implied by her name, and her readiness incites the question near the end of the story: "Why could we have not made of our ideals something constructive, taking from our experiences its creative force to bring to the world our loving attitudes?" (p. 193). This question foreshadows her decision to end her relationship with Jimson and to face her immediate future alone. Only in this way can she attain a personal awareness of her own emotional and rational integrity and allow this new awareness to guide her behavior.

The anguish that Ideal and Jimson experience because they have internalized stereotyped racial identities instead of accepting the responsibility of self-definition is duplicated in the reader's experience with the text. The novel provokes in the reader a tremendous sense of discomfort, uncertainty, and outright bewilderment because the process of reading the text reproduces the characters' own confusion, suffering, and ambivalence. Hence we confront the barrage of rhetorical, analytical discourse only to find our expectations for resolution repeatedly frustrated. For instance, early in the novel Ideal engages in a bout of paradoxical, self-recriminating analysis:

> Yes, I am going to tell you, warn you. This is Ideal. Look, take a good look. I am love gone wrong. I am that thing, whatever it is, which masquerades in the name of love. I am the mouth that seeks kisses for its own enjoyment— because it likes the liquid chasm. I am the woman who gives up nothing in the name of love, the woman who gives up what she lacks in order to gain what she does not know. I am all feeling, incapable of reason, mistaking kindness and sensuality for passion. With a warped vista and undisciplined flounderings, I relish the idea of marriage as living with God. (pp. 41-42)

Her monologue evokes Jimson's counterresponse about the inevitable dissolution of their relationship:

> Come on now, Ideal. . . . Come on, so that I can be left alone. I admit that I am weak, seduced by the moon. You could have helped me, though. You could have waited for me. I am out and I

know it. I would have come back. . . . You say that I have robbed you of your identity, that I stole your fire. Could it not be that we exchanged these things between us? If I do not accept the gift that you bring, the gift remains with you. Right now, I am unable to say what it is that I have taken from you. I have not opened the gift of you. The whole experience is intact. (p. 44)

Indeed, the entire novel evolves largely as a series of direct and indirect monologues and dialogues in counterpoint. If we are not to abandon the text as a confusing diatribe, we must struggle with it in order to push the process of reading beyond the familiar expectations of social realism and ready-made racial arguments in order to uncover perplexing questions about self-determination and personal freedom.

The Flagellants also flouts conventional expectations by not protesting against racial injustice in traditional ways. The central figures refuse to conform to heroic (and antiheroic) notions of black character portrayal, both of which assume idealized standards of behavior. Nor does analysis of their behavior advance racial arguments. Furthermore, these characters do not attempt to address white people in order to prove that racism is legally, morally, or ethically wrong—a departure from the works of three of the most famous twentieth-century black novelists: Richard Wright, Ralph Ellison, and James Baldwin. Instead of providing roles with which either white or black readers could easily identify, the text invites all readers to assume the roles of the central characters. In so doing the text demonstrates that the ready arsenal of racial arguments that Ideal and Jimson hurl at one another in order to justify their behavior are not merely inappropriate; they are, in fact, only convenient excuses that prevent them from realizing the personal freedom that they so desperately desire.

The novel suggests then that for many black Americans, like Ideal and Jimson, racial oppression is also self-inflicted. For them racism is not only the aggregation of genuine infringement of their civil liberties but, more importantly, also the daily by-product of their unconscious feelings of inadequacy which they internalize as racial inferiority. Rather than allow these feelings to emerge consciously and address them, some black people enact the racial myths and pass them around like symptoms of a contagious disease. As the disease spreads throughout the black population, those infected become increasingly and unwittingly complicit in perpetuating their own sense of subjugation. This is distressing news for people who believed that legislation would render them both equal to white Americans and free to choose the course of their own lives.

Throughout virtually its entire history, Afro-American literature has argued for the constitutional rights of black Americans. However, if this literature is to sustain a people in their efforts to secure not only civil liberty but personal liberty as well, it cannot focus on one to the exclusion of the other. Afro-American writing must dramatize *both* arguments for preserving the civil liberties of black people *and* appeals for the constructive exercise of their personal freedom. Black male writers have historically focused on dramatizing arguments about civil liberties, while contemporary black women writers are in the vanguard of depicting the quest for personal freedom. More recently, however, there has been a shift in the setting of recent black novels from public to private space, and conflict between a black man and white society has been supplanted by conflict between a black man and a black woman. Trying to determine whether one sex is more preoccupied with one type of freedom or whether one type of freedom is more important than the other is counterproductive. Both types of liberty are essential for a people to claim its freedom.

The Flagellants was one of the first novels to probe questions of freedom that lie outside the perimeter of civil liberties. Like Gayl Jones's *Corregidora* (1975), Toni Morrison's *The Bluest Eye* (1970), and Alice Walker's *The Third Life of Grange Copeland* (1970), this novel dramatizes complex questions of individual freedom and personal responsibility that belie traditional racial arguments. It is, as Mel Watkins accurately claimed, a precursor for the recent novels of black women writers.[8] Like most of these works, *The Flagellants* is set in intimate space, and it depicts black male brutality as a sign of the corruption of personal freedom.

Moreover, many of these works move beyond merely depicting the flawed alignment of freedom and brutality to celebrate the reformation of character in the so-called brutal male. Characters like Truman Held of Walker's *Meridian* (1977), Mister in her *The Color Purple* (1982), and Mut of Jones's *Corregidora* (1975; reprint 1986) consciously change their behavior toward their former victims. However, some critics have harshly criticized these works for their negative depictions of black men and have disregarded the healing power of transformation that is central to these works. A few critics have gone so far as to accuse many black women writers of either consciously or unconsciously evoking stereotyped images of black male brutality in exchange for the support of the white literary establishment.

It is too bad we cannot raise Zora Neale Hurston from the dead so that she might tell black writers and critics, male and female alike, that pursuing this charge is going to put them all into "a trick bag." Like Ideal and Jimson in *The Flagellants*, black writers and critics flagellate themselves with the very arguments they seek to refute. Rather than recognize their racial suffering as experiential knowledge, classify it, and heal its pain, they reduce it to rhetoric and scourge each other with circular recriminations.

Given this critical climate for black women's writing, it is no wonder that Polite cannot decide whether the new edition of *The Flagellants* is a curse or a blessing.[9] As a writer she must be pleased that her novel will have a new life; however, she must also have ambivalent feelings about the questionable privilege of having two sets of reviews. It is possible, even likely, that some of the new reviews will jump out of the "trick bag" of abstract rhetoric, easy analysis, and ready racial argument, and try to claim her novel as just another degrading depiction of black men. But ultimately it is more important for *The Flagellants* to have the opportunity to reach an entirely new readership, whose responsibility is to read the novel accurately. The new edition may not be an unqualified blessing for the author, but it is a blessing for both the book itself and its new audience.

Ideal's struggle is a difficult one. Trick bags abound. Indeed, her story stops when she sidesteps one trick bag and realizes that she—not Jimson, God, or the devil—must assume responsibility for transforming her life. She does not yet know how to create the life she desires; she therefore goes back in time in order to seek instructions from that period in her life when survival seemed more certain.

Ideal's fictive journey into the past is one form of a pattern that occurs in many recent novels by Afro-American women. Novels such as Angelou's *I Know Why the Caged Bird Sings*, Morrison's *The Bluest Eye* and *Sula*, and Shange's *Betsy Brown*, like *The Flagellants*, dramatize an abiding faith that the past holds a text that present-day readers must learn to interpret in order to move confidently and constructively into the future. The only literature that can assist a people in moving confidently and constructively into the future is an honest literature. For as the old folks have said, only the truth will set you free.

NOTES

I would like to thank Deborah McDowell; her thoughtful suggestions enhanced this introduction. The research for this introduction was made possible by support from the Faculty Research Program in the Social Sciences, Humanities, and Education at Howard University.

1. Mel Watkins, "Hard Times for Black Writers," *The New York Times Book Review* (22 February 1981), 3, 26-27. See also Nora Sayre, "Punishing," *The Nation* (9 October 1967), 334; Robert Ebert, "First Novels by Young Negroes," *The American Scholar* (Autumn 1967):682-84.

2. Frederick Raphael, "Jimson and Ideal," *The New York Times Book Review* (11 June 1967), 40.

3. William B. Hill, review of *The Flagellants* in *Best Sellers* (1 July 1967), 139-40.

4. Simpson's review appeared in the *New York Herald Tribune Book Week* (27 October 1963).

5. Stanley Kauffman, "Torn Loose," *The New Republic* (24 June 1967), 18 and 36.

6. Nikki Giovanni, review of *The Flagellants* in *Negro Digest* (January 1968), 97-98.

7. Zora Neale Hurston, *Their Eyes Were Watching God* (Urbana: University of Illinois Press, 1978), 286.

8. Mel Watkins, "Sexism, Racism and Black Women Writers," *The New York Times Book Review* (15 June 1986), 1, 35-37.

9. I would like to express my appreciation to Carlene Hatcher Polite, who spoke with me, by telephone, about her work on 2 March 1987. During this conversation, she expressed her ambivalence about the new edition of *The Flagellants*: "Like most writers, I am gratified to see the finished work, but I know, deep down, in me that I really don't care if I ever write another novel. I put my heart and my soul in

that one. . . . I appreciate Beacon Press for picking it up, but I don't know whether the new edition is a curse or a blessing."

BIBLIOGRAPHY

WORKS BY CARLENE HATCHER POLITE

The Flagellants. New York: Farrar, Straus and Giroux, 1967.

Sister X and the Victims of Foul Play. New York: Farrar, Straus and Giroux, 1975.

"Excerpt from *The Flagellants*." In *To Be a Black Woman: Portrait in Fact and Fiction*, edited by Mel Watkins and Jay David, 163–66. New York: William Morrow, 1970.

SECONDARY SOURCES

Ebert, Robert. "First Novels by Young Negroes." *The American Scholar* (Autumn 1967), 682–84.

Giovanni, Nikki. Review of *The Flagellants*. *Negro Digest* (January 1968), 97–98.

Hill, William B. Review of *The Flagellants*. *Best Sellers* (1 July 1967), 139–40.

Kauffmann, Stanley. "Torn Loose." *The New Republic* (24 June 1967), 18, 36.

Lottmann, Herbert R. "Authors and Editors." *Publishers Weekly* (12 June 1967), 20–21.

Raphael, Fredrick. "Jimson and Ideal." *The New York Times Book Review* (11 June 1967), 40.

Sayre, Nora. "Punishing." *The Nation* (9 October 1967), 334.

Schraufnagel, Noel. *From Apology to Protest: The Black American Novel*. De Land, Fla.: Everett/Edwards, 1973.

Watkins, Mel. "Hard Times for Black Writers." *The New York Times Book Review* (22 February 1981), 3, 26–27.

———. "Sexism, Racism and Black Women Writers. *The New York Times Book Review* (15 June 1986), 1, 35–37.

Worthington-Smith, Hemmett. "Carlene Hatcher Polite. "*Dictionary of Literary Biography XXXIII: Afro-American Fiction Writers after 1955*, edited by Thadious M. Davis and Trudier Harris, 215–18. Detroit: Gale Research, 1984.

The Flagellants

△

prologue

△

The afternoon is white. The earth is as quiet as the
snow. The few birds flying across the sky appear black
and free. Smoke from both my cigarette and incense
blow blue-gray forms into the silence. The lighting of
another cigarette has become a sort of ritual, a necessary

3

preface to my every act and sentiment. A blue-gray haze may be mistaken for my aura. I may be mistaken for a fool. The laughter that just permeated the room may be mistaken for gaiety. It is hysteria. The laughter's volume eases down into the same tone as the silence.

△

Long ago, in a room that was not quiet at all, a little girl was implored to dance atop a big brass bed. The guitar player's name was Black Cat. By morning, he was a junkman; by night, he was the moaning voice that sang away the pain of the room. The bold black outlines of the guests formed Matisse-like impressions against the wallpaper. The guests flowered, drooped, and wilted to the tones of the mournful man's guitar. A kerosene lamp cast a stationary black form onto the room's ceiling, so that each scene within the room was shadowed by its looming darkness. The lamp's candlepower was lost among the writhings of the guests. Only one object in the room grasped the lamplight—the big brass bed.

"I want to go home," hollered the little girl.

The child's body was fixed in an arc that might have been the initial movement for the requested dance. One of her hands grasped and held together the woman's nightgown that she wore. A blackbird in snow tracks the same patterns as she did atop the big brass bed that night. Every color within the room hurled challenges across the bed. Every moan and coaxing cheer whirled through the confines of the room. The stationary form could no longer contain the strain of the child's protest or the noise of the scene. The guests emerged from the wallpaper. The mournful man stopped whin-

4

ing the blues. The guitar leaned against the chair. The little girl wiped her tears and said farewell.

"Goodbye and God be with ye . . ." She was outside that house, the last house of her great-grandmother. The great-grandmother took the child's hand, walked around the corner, down the street to the house where the child was born. For the last time the old woman, warped and reduced by slavery, would lead the child. With an ancient and tired breath she said:

"Remember now what I tell you, Ideal. Always walk tall. Never bow down to anything or to anyone; unless, of course, you feel like bowing—quite naturally, you will then . . . I never will know what possessed your mother to give you such a name, child."

A low laugh let go of the old woman's face. She smiled at the infinite thought the name provoked.

Ideal looked more the spectator than the inhabitant of the quarter. Her dress was stark white against the looming shadows. Her hair was dressed with the same severity, braided into two long braids. The looming shadow colored her skin, so that one was unable to determine if it were brown, or orange, or yellow, or white. It was just flesh—all shining, blackened softly by her frown. She looked up at the stunted slave woman. The questions in Ideal's eyes were too magnificent to be answered. It was the common, intimate question that is at the bottom of all our hearts . . . What did walking tall mean? What did bowing have to do with feeling? What would bowing before something or someone do to the heart of the bower? The great-grandmother's heart had answered these questions a long time ago.

5

Ideal felt an agitation in the old lady's hands. They were black and shriveled. Leather was more supple. The hard time had etched its rough history into those hands. The hands were no longer capable of gesturing and caressing—only clutching . . . Ideal pulled tightly against the fragile force of the woman. She listened to the sound of their walking. The sound echoed somewhere in that space which seemed to be just a step ahead of them. Ideal, letting go the old woman's hand, ran ahead trying to outdo her own shadow.

"Wait, now. Don't try to get ahead of me or yourself," warned the woman.

They walked past the corner church that was still and empty of sinners. Only one word of a sign inviting the people to attend the church's daily services to God remained—"Hell." Ideal had gone one stifling summer night to visit the church when her great-grandmother had wanted to witness the baptismals. The heat, that night, easily goaded the witnesses into believing that they were dwelling in purgatory and totally incapable of ever escaping their burning burdens. Cardboard fans, donated by the community's undertaker, were provided so that the hot air might be stirred along. The fans bore a picture of a little girl with long curls, a pretty straw hat, and white gloves. Under the picture were the name and location of the undertaker and a sentimental phrase regarding his sense of condolence and practice. It was difficult for Ideal to reconcile the pretty, smiling-faced little girl with dying and graveyards.

The four walls of the church embraced and unified sinners, seekers, the bemoaned and the beloved. Over

6

the altar was a *Pietà*. The Christ figure before the congregation's eyes was painted pink. His forsaken eyes were painted blue. The blood dripping from his wounds was tear-stained and faded by the ecstatic people who used the painted wall to receive their plaints and affirmations. In front of the wailing wall was a hinged, raised platform which seemed to have been constructed hurriedly by some crude carpenter who knew not the honor and antiquity of his calling. The church's choir stood upon the platform. The satin-robed singers, swaying from side to side and rocking each board of the syncopating, scrubbed floor, sang the gospel over and over until the singsong sound of goodness swelled the witnesses' heads, moving the congregation in its entirety to plead that the song let them go. The House of God was fired with powerful babel. The entire quarter was there that night . . . stars and dust. Sprinklings of language, unknown tongues, consumed the witnesses into pews of tears. The Lord have Mercy, screeching emotions swooped down across them, making them lift their tearful feet out of the dust. The dust streamed into mud and clay. The people had come to petition, to request, to implore the Good Lord. Joining together to manifest their God consciousness, the people, reflecting all truth, made pristine and chromatic the scale of their true colors.

"But do you know who you are?"

"Yes! we do."

Insults, outrages, maniacal bellows of ancient, now wrecked myths, allowed them to know on that stifling summer night.

7

"Shall I help you?" asked a bass voice.

"If you can," answered a contralto.

"Trace down this tree. Let me show you men in its stead. Leaf through this bush, extinguish the burning fire . . ."

The great-grandmother fanned herself feverishly. Ideal braced herself against the uncomfortable wooden bench. Through the congregation's center, the raucous message pierced a shaft of light. They became a community of one heart left wide open for a shepherd's healing touch. The doors of the church opened. Their pastor, the preacher of the little corner church, stood tall and smiling. He outstretched his arms and seemed to embrace individually the whole neighborhood of souls. The choir burst into song. He began his way down the aisle of the little church toward the chair on the platform that was fashioned and reserved for him.

I Am hath sent me unto you . . .

The fire was out. The wailings stopped. The air filled with laughter and greetings. The cardboard fans waved him on his way. By name, he called out to his members as he passed. The people loved the man who moved past them with a kingly walk, a giant's will. He mounted the platform and stood—all smiling, dazzling with love. "God, bless . . . ," he said quietly and took his chair upon his throne. He was a tall, magnificent man with a smile that caused the sun to take heart. Ideal's great-grandmother was forever raving about his good looks, wondering if his teeth were his own or false. She thought them too straight, white, perfect, and even to be his own. He was a chocolate brown man and,

8

of course, looked good enough to eat. The good sisters of the little corner church devoured him with their stares, masticated upon his good word, nudged out their responses with smacks of a digested Amen. Ideal moved to the edge of her seat and strained her neck above the witnesses blocking her view. The light from a diamond ring he wore played upon the walls. The brilliance enchanted Ideal. In her child's mind, she was unable to determine if he were a flesh-and-blood man or a figment of the people's need. The message he preached that stifling summer night would haunt and challenge the child forever. The doctrine of catapulting one's wishes and thoughts beyond that volition with which a grasshopper is endowed struck the intuitive wisdom of the child. If his wise and biblical language were on a level beyond her grasp, she was able to perceive the image of the grasshopper. She would be forever in search of the giant's will . . .

His being changed from smiling to sweating. His voice boomed curses and disciplines down upon the heads of the beholders. He preached, sang, moaned, and cried to the Good Lord. His body was erect and dead center, walking, hopping, dancing in his ecstasy. The congregation was carried away with the power and intelligence of the preaching man. His breath begged for air, rattled with each word pouring from his mouth. The people, fused with his being, prayed that he not stop. The choir began chanting in time with his rhythm. The organ filled the little church with the beat of his heart, so that his voice resounded under them, over them, penetrating their feelings with the spirit. The fire was leaping from the bush, searing the eyes of the believers. In the moment, the good brothers and sisters of the church whooped and hollered for release. Up on their feet, their bodies contracted and released all agony and salt. A woman in back of Ideal sprang up, jerking and groaning in an unknown tongue. Ideal was petrified by the quivering sight of the spasmodic woman. Bench sharers attempted to quieten her. They wrestled with either a spirit who had entered the woman or a devil seeking delight. In the commotion, the woman's necklace was torn from her throat. Ideal was baptized by a cascade of flung pearls. The spirit broke loose from the rafters, raining down upon the witnesses in the form of public repentance, promises of changed ways, skepticism, ice-cold stares. The commotion repeated its pearl casting in every corner. The great-grandmother hugged Ideal close to her bosom, covered the child's eyes, so that she might not see. The pastor led the people on. They convulsed and responded with a common will. His feet thudded on the hollow pulpit. Wild with the feeling, his eyes gazed past the rafters toward the heavens. His vision tore itself from its sockets. He was gone now . . . His arms turned into wings. He flapped and lighted, fluttered, strutted, spinning dervish whirls up and down the platform. Two men moved forward in order to bring back the preaching man. Ideal wanted to know what had happened. Surely, he must be dying. They grabbed his arms and whispered calm words. Ideal could see the consciousness settling back down into his body. The men let go. The preacher had returned to the realm of the living. He stood soaking wet with unembarrassed sweat. Smiling, the church became luminous with his light. Yes, he was their man, their living symbol of the giant's will. He had come from the Bottom as they had, witnessed the bedrock the same as they. He talked their language and played their games. He could sit wretched and forsaken on a bedside bemoaning ignorance and love's outcome. His cries had torn the hurt from his eyes and dammed the tears that wished for a place to lie down and flow. Somewhere along the periphery of all pain, the wish for what-ought-to-be must lie . . . Tongues can reach feelings where words dare not. Words can reach feelings lodged in the limbs of the people. The people were convulsed out of themselves, entirely, that stifling summer night. They were transcended into states where, God knows, the divine must dwell. Quite frankly, their ears heard a whole scale of breath and tone . . . The choir disappeared from the platform. The great floor unhinged. The preacher descended. Candidates for baptismal marched single file down the aisle. Down into the blackness they walked. The waters splashed drops of sweat and tears. The drops rose up, splintering, bursting into multicolored bubbles. Wrapped in white shrouds, the candidates ascended from the depth—wringing wet. They were born again, mumbling virgin vows, sobbing, bowing at the feet of our crucified Christ. Ideal could not distinguish the difference between the cry of joy and the cry of pain. Both were formidable. Where was the God who had created the flowers, the light, the heart of this place called Black Bottom? Who was the God who had chosen our mothers to bring us into the world? Where was the

God who is love? Who was this painted pink Christ with blue eyes? Who was this Christ whose Father chose to rain down high water? The child cried tears of ignorance. Her great-grandmother continued leading her home past the little corner church.

"Don't step on that thing, girl," the old woman warned. "There is no telling what it might be. You know how that old woman Beata Thangbee is. She is likely to have put some conjure there—just to bother some poor soul as it passed by. She is the most evil thing I think I have ever laid eyes upon."

Beata Thangbee's house stood divided from the church by a vacant lot. People in the Bottom referred to any uninhabited, grassless, lifeless piece of land as vacant. As soon as the sun was up and shining, neighbors came in droves to Beata's house. Several were waiting as Ideal and the old woman passed. They would wait there until Beata called out their turn to come inside and talk to her. She listened to the dreams, nightmares, and visions that had tortured or comforted the people during the night. Those who were waiting had fallen to the bottom of their dreams. Waiting until the sun came up would be too long for them. It was best to come now, to wait. Beata advised them through some inherited and self-appointed sense of wisdom and knowledge of God's will.

If talking to them were not enough, she was able to administer oils, ointments, potions for whatever it was that ailed them. If her words could not be fathomed, she gave them numbers to identify their happy and wretched dreams. All could be helped who came to

12

Beata. Ideal smelled the oily, incensed mood of the house.

Another vacant lot had to be passed. This one was the never-never land of Ideal's play. She pretended that the hard yellow mud of the lot was a field of flowers. Broken glass reflected colors as wild as make-believe flowers. Only debris and junk were able to vegetate in the lot. Ancient garbage dumps had become unconquerable mountains. She climbed atop the mound and looked for the new world. Her eyes refused to see time and bits of uprooted things. They went on past a run-down barn. The great-grandmother gave her a moment to peek in and see a horse that slept there. The horse belonged to Mr. Coffee, a vagrant citizen of the Bottom. At daybreak the mangy horse was dragged out and hitched to a wagon. Mr. Coffee was a ragman by trade. Ideal could never understand why discarded clothes and dirty rags were of interest to the man. When he returned at the end of day, the barn filled with people who grabbed among the rags, looking for clothes that only the rich would call by the name of rag. A pitchfork rested against the barn's wall. Someone had told Ideal that the fork belonged to the devil. Everyone knew that the devil was a permanent resident walking, talking, visiting freely among the dwellers.

Ideal and the old woman took a short cut through tall weeds that twisted around their legs.

"That's the devil trying his best to keep us from going on, child," the woman reckoned.

The weeds whipped Ideal's legs until their color was drained. They bled little drops of blackish-red blood.

13

Sunflowers' foreboding faces dropped seeds onto the earth. The wind scattered one of the seeds upon a festering rat swarming with maggots. Would a flower bloom? Ideal needed to know . . . They reached home. Bottom dwellers referred to each other as "home." "Hey, home, what's happening?" "You'd better believe, home, that I am looking good."

At the top of the steps was the door that closed out the Bottom. Behind that door was the way of Ideal's life. Her great-grandmother refused to climb the stairs.

"Too old for all that huffing and puffing," she complained. "I'll see you in my dreams, dear heart."

The house and its inhabitants were asleep. The child hurried into the toilet—closet would be more descriptive. It would have been impossible to stretch out and die there. The chipped, green painted walls sweated a moist substance. It was easy to become toilet trained in this closet—in that the oozing substance stimulated the system to rebuff, if nothing more. The kitchen was just outside the closet door. It shined with greased odors of food. Soul food, it was called. The smell of it served as a character analysis for the dwellers. By sniffing its aromas, they could tell from which part of the South one had come and, more importantly, the price that had been paid for one's sustenance. Only landlords and successful wrongdoers could afford the best.

On occasion, the hunches, worrisome dreams, and comic-strip perusals of the empty-pocketed indigents parlayed digits from one to ten into streaks of good luck that cautiously dropped them a bag of fresh money for their daily preoccupation with policy and the numbers.

14

Ideal got into bed quickly, pulling the covers over her head. She had to close out the coaxing guests, the memory of the jumping church, Beata, the seed of her great-grandmother. The child's mind went out. The world became pitch-and-red jangles of spiraling symbols and ricocheting lines. And then the smell came crawling out of the walls. Ideal was up on her knees, searching out, feeling up and down the wall, chasing across the pillow, lifting the mattress, striking matches, setting fire to the bedsprings, squashing the crawling smell. Bedbugs, too, dwelled in the Bottom. They visited by night, in darkness, in crevices preserving the rock-bottom antiquity. Someday, Ideal would learn that a bed is for other reasons than cowering in the dark. The old folks said that they didn't sleep; instead, they simply suffocated in their nighttime hiding from crawlers and haunts.

In the child's dream, a glazed green boy with an iridescent mouth laughed like a hyena. He had a pale doll upon his head. Ideal recognized it as her first baby doll. Its blond hair flopped against his glistening green face. He giggled and clowned his way toward the hysterical, dreaming child. His muted laughter mouthing a shining red shape constrained his meaning. As he reached toward the wreck of Ideal to reveal his truth—why he, of all symbols, had creeped out of mind to become an unidentifiable memory—day broke. Sunlight fought him out of mind and back into his residing space in the wall. It was day, thank God, moving day.

Some unknown force had listened in on the prayerful mourners.

"If you will just give us the strength to endure . . ."

Ideal was granted permission to go downstairs and have her last look at the place where she had come into the world. The Bottom was her first glimpse. The tones she heard became her mother language. The beliefs she overheard became her first fear. She would remember these sounds and images for the rest of her life. They were her roots. She would retain this life in that part of her mind that dwelled deep within her eyes—behind a frown. The images would become less distinct with time, but she would be colored by them until her dying day. The child's head would carry the candy store where she bought stale, imitation watermelon slices, double-dip ice cream cones. She hated imitation fruit, wax flowers. Perhaps because one day she had spied a luscious-looking piece of fruit, reached for the offered apple, only to find out that it was unreal. The woman offering the wax fruit doubled up with laughter at the sight of the child's disillusion.

This same woman played another indelible joke upon Ideal. The funny woman enjoyed the reputation of being down to earth, filled with motherwit. She advised Ideal's mother to keep a close eye on the child, to watch every move she made. In watching Ideal's growing, she saw that she was beautiful, an unusual child, and that if she stayed on the right track, she would become this same kind of woman. She prescribed that the only way to control a child of Ideal's looks and temperament was to lay down the law, demand that she walk a chalked line. She predicted that unless the child had the devil beaten out of her constantly, her high-strung and willful nature would be her ruination.

The applied advice sprouted a self-destroying root at the bottom of the poor child's free heart. Punishment became the cockeyed plumb line by which the depth of love could be measured and angled—a divining rod . . . It was a sign of evil to possess the nerve to fight back, to defend one's nature. She was bullied for her cowardice, chastised for being softhearted. Yes, she was glad to be moving away from this hurting root. The creed of the Bottom was rendered indelible. The scenes and joys would be forgotten. Perhaps, fleeting images are all that the heart can bear.

She would remember the corner poolroom which coronated a daily king. The men played the game with a desperation equal to out-and-out war. Inez had to be remembered. She was slashed to her bloody, unsolved death while the whole neighborhood slept. Not one soul claimed to be a witness; but all of them could tell the number of razor marks that changed her sleeping body into a canvas sack of blood-red ribbons. Inez had hollered out the window at a zooming car. She cursed Ideal for being an utter fool, but she saved her life from being cut down by an ignorant fool with a Ford V-8. The first feel of death she would remember—and the man across the street who caught rain water to wash away the devil who hardened his bones. The devil possessed Red John, too, who drank plenty whisky and housed pretty women. It was said that one of these ladies had a temper equal to Red John's and delighted in throwing clay bricks to prove it. Stone drunk and off somewhere on a tangent, she pelted Signor Paresiani, causing him to walk with an innocent limp. Red John went scot-free, laughed at her error. Her whisky had not let her tell one from the other. Yes, Ideal would remember Red John. She had sat on the bottom step daydreaming, watching the world go by.

Red John gave chase after a playful man. At a moment in which they chased past Ideal, the right hand of Red John became level with her eyes. Automatically, blindly, wrapped up in his dynamic sham, he whipped out a switch blade, and ran jokingly by. Reflex, only, saved her sight. It was the habit of Bottom men to play in such dynamic fashion. "I'll kill you, niggah!" was a war cry when heard outside the Bottom. When spoken to each other, this same violent affirmation was a statement of love and blood's identity. But the people would allow no one else to take this freedom.

She would remember the neighborhood idiot. Maybe he was intelligent. The neighbors did not give him the right to find out. Anyone who was born with a head that size had to be filled with water rather than brains. The beer garden that housed or threw out Saturday night revelry, the tradition of the night's enchantment had to be remembered; and the blacksmith who was white in spite of the heat igniting the noise of his clanking sound—the church's backyard barbecues and ice cream churnings . . . Cleo must have been a direct result of the rape of the ancient continent. She stood seven feet tall, grinned, guzzled cheap wine and cursed her husband from sunup to sundown. Cleo could not bear to have the man out of her sight. Please do not look at him. She beat him unmercifully for being handsome enough to be desired. She would remember the champion in Joe Louis, the parade and good time that broke loose in the streets as soon as the radio announced, "And still the heavyweight champion of the world . . ." It was only necessary to hear the second word spoken— "still." This was enough to telegraph the uproar that followed.

Frog rigged up his tightrope. He had worked during his boyhood in the South with a roadside carnival. Some European circus performer had taught him his prize feat. He walked high above the crowd while the onlookers stood below supporting and cheering both Joe Louis and him. The Champion's glory was grand enough to be shared. She would remember Halloween and that, in the Bottom, this night was reserved for the play of grown folks who dressed the part of their wildest dreams and frightened children and tickled each other. The people blackened their faces with cold stove smut and masqueraded as the character who played most deeply upon their hearts. Women chose to dress as men. The men chose to dress as vagabonds. Telling who was who and why became an exercise, a delightful game.

Ideal got up from the step, snapped out of her nostalgic mood. She walked back to the vacant lot, her lot. She stopped and leaned against the back corner of a house. This same corner had hidden from the eyes of the people a feeling that Ideal rejected as mysterious and foreboding. The feeling had been pushed against her, rubbed against her while her mouth was kissed and her ears received whispers of "Don't you tell . . ." Some warm quality of this experience gushed out of the child's mouth as a misleading sigh. She disliked not the

19

rubbing, but rather, the taboo restrained in its slither. "I don't care who you go and tell," the boy told her. "Well, I am going to tell that you were doing something bad to me."

Once more Bottom thought welled up into her mind. God was vengeful, night was steaming with witches, everything came out to crawl, the devil stalked the land, good feelings were the result of listening to his charm. It was not right to feel alive, warm, or free. The presence of God would only be recognized through suffering the weight of a bloody cross which had been fashioned in a time before our appearances to coincide with our earthly measurements. The parallel was no longer than one's outstretched arm span. The perpendicular was no longer than one's true height. No one could see it, but they all knew it was obligingly being worn. The word had been passed around that it was the mode.

"Where you are going now, Ideal, you will have to act and talk just like white folks; because if you don't, God will strike you dead."

"What's wrong with the way I talk and act? God gave me my voice, my ways. The white people living down here talk and act just like us. You are just jealous because you are not moving away."

"No, I am not either! I'm going to stay down here in the Bottom all my life. If God had wanted me to be in some other place, he would have had me to be born in some other place."

Staying next door to white people was the same as staying next door to black people, yellow people, brown people, any people. They cried the same blues, the same joys, ate, slept, had babies and funerals, went their merry and tragic ways. Simplicity, the sole quality of poverty, ignores the complexities of the disparate society. Analysis of the poor condition is directed toward how to survive, overcome. The same door never opens at the same time for anyone. Some doors never open for colored people, for discolored people, for men, women, children, idiots, wise men, for anyone . . . The door chooses its own knockers. It opens upon the word.

one

△

The wind pushed the door. Ideal noticed it, but did
nothing to stop the back-and-forth slamming. Counting
the pauses between noise and silence was far less nerve-
racking than digging up the past. Ideal welcomed anything that could aggravate her paralysis, conjure her

senses into unstringing an aimless pain. Crouching between dream and fact, unraveling filaments of piqued senses, seeking visions to condone sluggishness, had become therapeutic actions for the hysterical young woman. She crawled into the middle of the bed, draped the cover over her god-forsaken, eternally cold feet. Covering her head was no longer imperative.

The bed consumed three quarters of the room. You had to go to bed if you stayed in this room. Lie down. Gaze out the window at a brick wall. Look down the air shaft. The room was decorated to tease the sun. The walls were chalk white. One wall contained something more—a gigantic, yellow-orange sun. The sun's myriad light rays were fashioned with a palette knife so that each ray's apex displayed a conical form which gyrated the viewer's eye from periphery to dead center, then back to periphery again. Color overpowered the cracked plaster nest. The mirrored door across from the head of the bed reflected an aura of ragged-edged rust.

What am I doing to myself? I have become suspicious, even of wish. What has interceded to detain me and, in the same breath, advise me? It would have been less painful to have never questioned a shadow intruding upon the sun. Our beings goad us into assuming the role of whip wielder. Our ignorance oppresses us, hammers us back down into our assaulted root. Causality flowers us into penitent switches. Violence is the fruity thrill. Passion, transmitting a staccato beat, kicks our moaning tone from spontaneous curse to intuitive slang. We immerse philanthropic goodness in a bucket of blood, daring it to stretch out its hand and holler for help.

I was willing that the end come as a retributive act committed against myself, but now I am subjected to another's will. This other will possesses the diabolical cleverness to get under my skin, to undermine me with dispassionate thought, indisputable reason. I wanted to be beaten down by my own distrustful nature, to be relieved of the responsibility of the quest. The trappings have dazzled me away from the freedom to choose independently the way out. I answer, "Yes, I will," to instructions and gouge my eyes out desiring what I do not want at all. The original design for the game's end, surely, would have contained some element of divinity. In which part of the linkage did the rust first begin to show? What was the first unhinged squeak to disrupt the quiet and leave me the slothful pariah who contemplates nothingness and bellows at ceilings?

Ideal squinted at the stark whiteness. Life had become a Southern custom of decorative little window shades pulled down against the sun. The dark would free her from the light. Everyday shadows spotted the wall and darted across the gigantic sun. She performed the cigarette-lighting ritual, turned to the mirror to begin the labyrinthine mouthful she was preparing for Jimson.

Here I am with the all day, the walls, the grub, life's wind from a window, feeling sorry for myself. My parole is a night out, a flat drink, a hot-aired movie, heads of people. Yours is the competitive condition, the constriction, the futility, the beaten path. Your night out is a cathartic drunk to the point of disease.

Tragedy nurtures us, leads us. We wear it as a great mantle, commit the vilest acts, perceive the most divine notions under its seedy, threaded lining. We talk fast,

24

directly to the heart, pull out the dreamed-of-one-morning silver rapier, commanding it to let blood. The command is that the pulse pulsates, the lip quivers, the arm embraces, the heart loves, that IT lives.

The master stands hip high in a puny pus, baptizing slaves, while we cower behind flesh masks watching them lose face. Judgment fills our contemptuous attitudes as we see slaves sprinkled with negation, resignation, improbability, and somnolence. We are dazed by this lovely ritual, this mysterious manifestation. We do not question for fear of ridicule, ludicrousness, unfoundedness. "Get my faith," the master advises. "Have faith. Do not doubt. You are not supposed to understand. Accept." But how when I allow my mind to pursue its jungle wildness? . . . Consolation from a lover? Now, really . . . His truth comes out so feebly with its eye turned toward the blank. I should expect one to be crazed by its almighty lash.

The master's lying revelation hangs the head and purifies poison with its breathlessness. "You will understand," he consoles, "someday." There is a universe toward whom that same hopeful discipline is directed. "But this is good for you, the only way. Just snap, bend, doubt not, love, trust, obey, emulate, do, do, do." He forgives himself his atrocities; for he is courting progress, democratic process, selecting his privileged choices, bedeviling his flagellants—while protecting us from the same. Drafting the enslaved to defend him, he begs to be quickened for his calling to save mankind from dogmatic injustice.

Myself, I must realize to be transient, to be womb, the caul which breaks sending forth into the world eyes . . .

And now, you of all people, Johnny, Jack, Richard, Ben, Peter, Henry, Allen—Jesus! Sometimes I do not even know whom I am talking to. And I know your name as well as I know my own; but it is battered around on my tongue and falls out as anybody's name. Anyway, you understand, my Father . . . You dictate that I must worship head high at the prefabricated shrine. In my constant bass voice, I ask myself, "Am I being tricked?"

It is taken for granted that we are brutally enlightened. "Indulge us, please, be patient" is the pardoning axiom. Vanity makes us daily violate ourselves. We have come to suspect blackness. It has affected us, so that in each moment we live we see the foul-mouthed lie. The chase after the alternative contains all and nothingness, black and white, punishment and beatification. What shall we hold up before ourselves? We do not sense straight for hurt and pity.

Honest labor shall pay us back. Money affords expectation, confidence, faithful production, and substitutes loving by giving. But I, too, like the feel of the mantle, Jimson; the fancy of being aware of the irrationality, the madness I am capable of attaining, the squalor in which I can adjust and lie, the bloody ax I can wield, the shame through which I can radiantly smile, the wearing of a scent that mutes a violated body's stench, the pride that can be painted on to cheat the hunger out of mouths . . . Thoughts shall question me until I lose my mind. No longer can I reshape myself submissive, mold myself resilient for another's evil. Mine has taken such a pound. We must hold out, and daily receive all that is done against us, all that we do unto ourselves. We are at pleasure only when we wish; but then the paradox cajoles again, and we wind up wishing even during pleasure. I should like to run up against that wall, batter it, stop, turn around, deliver one final curse, grovel across the earth sucking after one fleck of truth, swallow, smile; then fade away before my very senses. I can, but I will not. I cannot take people. I cannot take me. I am afraid to think on that one act that will forever relieve me.

Jimson, you beautiful black man, we cannot stay it. It is so much more natural being ignorant and forsaken, deceived and handicapped, poetic and slobbering; and speculating upon that ecstatic writhing which sends us formless. We have finished with greater pride, greater distrust, soothing ourselves on an indifference for a mankind toward which we cannot manifest love. Nothing has forced or found our good.

I cook slop, keep a dirty house, wear hand-me-down clothes. Vermin maintain a perpetual sentry across the kitchen floor, under the pipe-leaking sink. Crusts of substandard life refuse to budge from under my toenails. I feel the sunlight and imagine one day I will wheel us out into the just life. Then this incarnation can be exploited as soul, as a past, as something to be thankful for, as a gauge toward attainment, as the surmounted obstacle. What makes me know that one day the sum of all this will diminish and leave total sun?

"Why do you not take that infernal good look at yourself and discover IT; then, it could be largely what you make it," said the looking-glass seer wiping off her crystal ball with her hoary sleeve.

27

"What do you make of all this I have been running down to you?" I asked.

"Don't dote on it, forget it, transcend it, live your life, take faith, love, forgive," she said.

"What shall be its guise next time—in the name of faith?"

"Oh shit," she said, receding into the mirror.

"Wait a minute," I said, "let's start this flux over from the beginning." And I wind up rounding up the dizzying air, seeking a way to make one bloody assault, to expectorate one virulent spit—going mad awaiting rebirth.

"But you can find it only through yourself . . ."

Ideal, pondering the looking-glass seer's snaggled tooth, gate-mouthed wisdom, quizzically laughed, and called back to her with the same.

Jimson would be home soon to receive the daily tirade. Through him, the inadequate, lopsided protest would gather momentum, manly deduction. Profundity flared up through his pointed finger. Foot tappings, beard strokings, noddings, pitying head shakings, complemented his sagacity. His posture would coax the rehearsed lines into combustible appearances. Ideal lay waiting for the time when it would be out in the open, when she would be carried away playing the savage, versed witch. Anxiety blinked colored spots before her eyes, flapped the window shade, streamed from her armpit. Gas bubbles bounced in the void. She had succeeded again. Her mind had re-entered the whip handle. Punishment lay entangled under matted blankets sighing whimpers reserved for neglected children, mistreated dogs. For saturation's sake! go to sleep.

△

Sulphur clouds warned the painted sun. A blackbird signaled a pack of albino wolves. An instant screech of yellow light exploded into walking fire. Flames gutted a mud staircase, leaving a gaudy corridor with ashen steps. Doors began to appear through the panic—out of every crevice. A paper serpentine crawled across the doors excreting "EXIT" from its dragging tail. Attached to the end of its tail was a final door preening luminous in its knowledge that it was the way. The knowledge was the effect of being no more than the door that was most unattainable to the walking fire. The air would be life's breath on the other side of the door. The light would be one's first glimpse of the radiant universe. Ideal twisted and turned. She fought to come up to the door, to land on the other side, to stay on the side once she was awake. One eye opened. She was still in the middle of the bed. She could hear Jimson whistling to himself. The slamming door opened wider. The wind was cool and eerie. She yanked the cover from her feet, trying to cover the rest of her body. The wind moved down her ears, across her face, through her hair. It was overtaking her. She was dreaming. She knew it. She was awake. She felt it. The wind whirled the tenets of witches and horror down into the bottom of her being. Ideal could not recover. She had to call out, to call Jimson. Make him take away this god-awful mess. His name would not push past her teeth. Freedom was locked inside her head. The fire flattened the blackbird into a bantam-cock weather vane that fluttered its smoking wings, commanding the wolves to singe the sun. The paper serpentine found fault with itself, unhinged the final door, and defaced the wall of the gaudy corridor with the message "I spy the Boom-a-Rye." The sun dripped feathers down the yellow light shaft. The feathers bore the numbers nine-one-four. Transformed into an upside-down chair, the four scattered the remains of the featherless bird. The one firing sparks knelt in the ashes searching for its horizontal equivalent. "Moan, Ideal, moan. Don't let those witches ride across your head like that. Stand up! Shout, girl, shout!" The nine kept insisting it was the Triad Triumphant thrice come.

Salvation slapped Ideal out of bed and sent her flying through the apartment, overturning chairs, searching under pillows, tearing through the closet, feeling along the bookshelves, patting down the curtains, calling out to Jimson, looking for him, imploring him not to play games.

Jimson was not playing games . . . He was walking down the hall with his Jimson's-coming-home-now stride; whistling his poignant tune, jingling his keys, unlocking the door. Ideal welcomed the hulk as an apparition. The flesh Jimson was playing hide-and-seek somewhere in the apartment. The apparition spoke, "No, Ideal, you would not believe me if I told you that I knew you were having your dream, that I came as soon as I could." This was not the first time Jimson had witnessed the moaning anguish of his woman. The first time, he thought Ideal was playing a joke on him, testing the depth of his aroused sleep, his capacity to sense her thought and need.

"Come on, now, Ideal, snap out of it. You know how I hate that infernal dream of yours. It's all right now. Your man is here."

"Oh Jesus, Jimson, I cannot stand it. Every time I leave my door open, that dream enters. Once, I asked my mother what it meant. The old-fogy reason she gave me describes the sensation perfectly. She said the old folks call it 'witches riding.' It's true, Jimson, that is precisely what it is. I can feel the wind riding softly over my head, blowing its blurred message down my ear. I realize I am dreaming, but I cannot fully awaken myself. I can hear those hideous, inhuman cries coming out of my head, but my protest is smothered by the pillow. A bantam-cock feather begins to itch my last vestigial nerve. Oh, God . . . it is too much. I have been having this dream for years. It's funny, though, that it never happens if the door is fully open, but only when I am stupid enough to leave the door standing cracked. Will you take me out for a drink as soon as I can get up and get myself together?"

△

The bar was empty when Jimson and Ideal arrived. They had begun coming earlier in the day, now that they did not need the affirmation of the crowd, or seek an audience that would appreciate their being lovers. They had enjoyed being unveiled, shining with adoration and affinity. Now they understood each other's needs, quiet. They did not speak to communicate, touch to feel, or dance across the sawdust . . . any more.

"We are not made for this world, Ideal. This is not our time. You belong to the world of wafting incense and smoky tea, the world of white and ivory. You are my lover from the pages of books. You are too fragile to love me right now."

The bartender wiped the ring the glass had stamped upon the bar. The ring gave her mouth the impetus to form from its wet impression—a sigh.

"It's over, Jimson, I know it. Over as contained in the glass's wet ring. That's silly and a coward's foolish way to say it to you, isn't it? But you know how cowardly I am. Only you have made me stand up in the world and tell them all that I am—I beg your pardon—was in love. I still cannot believe it. We may as well stop our performance. Let's play to an empty house. Remember the times when we were gleaming with our light and love? We sought crowds that would readily see that we were in love. We listened for their applauding comments. Remember the cleaved warmth we left on the subway seats, park benches, bar stools? We played our roles beyond the cinematic dimension. The public properties of lovers achieved full utility when we bowed to the call. Now, we have unmasked each other and pointed up our undoing souls."

"Yes, we were love, Ideal. We still are. We are separate now, that's all. One would think that you have absorbed nothing of our time together, girl. Don't you ever take time to read my books; do you merely dust them? Impermanence is the law of the universe. We have saturated, mastered each other through understanding. We have talked too much. I have been trying to get this through your head. Nothing in life stays the same. Our first breath is our last. We are born and daily become dead, unborn."

"Please don't talk now. I want to hurry and cry before the crowd gets here. You know that I don't want them to see the affirmation of nothingness in our faces. Remember how we met, Jimson? We were something grand, something too, too beautiful. Remember the times when we could dance all night long? Those were the days when the Village was an institution, a city unto itself, the unofficial borough. Then came the invasion of the poetry-and-jazz boys who masturbated onstage, choking to death on toilet paper scrolls of pronouncements unfit for bordellos. Waiting their turns to appear, they scribbled spontaneous poems to the tones of their newly found idols. And please don't forget the part-time beats arriving from Canarsie, getting their acts together down in the subway station. A sign painter could have become rich painting signs for them that broadcasted how hip they were—because they smoked pot . . .

"What is this green-backed monstrosity, this stainless-steel erection, this glorified commune? The buildings are cleaned with Brillo. Probably, the people must agree to sign over their names and call themselves by numbers when they lease those characterless idiot boxes. Aw hell, yes, I love a Mies van der Rohe, a Le Courbusier, a Saarinen, a Frank Lloyd Wright; but, these boys designing the buildings that are cropping up down here now are contractors not architects. So many square rooms for so many square feet. The Green Flower was the place to go, the hangout. Remember it was so crowded, we had to dance back to back, belly to belly, side to side, inside your coat, under your hat; just so long as we could keep on dancing, do it up brown. Two or three people might have been wedged in between us, but who cared as long as we all kept the place swinging. Ray Charles was just beginning to be the man in New York. How many times was there a scene started by some weird drunk's mumbling that he had had too much of *Having a Woman Away 'Cross Town?* I never will forget the night the leather-jacket boys decided to look me over, daring you to object, silently threatening you with their mock force. They had me scared, though, with their brink-of-war strategy; but you won, you outstared them. They did nothing but sneaked away into the thick funk. When we got outside, remember, they were having a snowball fight? Wasn't it that winter's first snow? And Jimson, no one in New York knows Central Park any better than we do. I never knew it was so enormous, or had so many green grass laps and fade-aways that you cannot reach from here . . . You lose New York completely—the noise, grime, people, anything you want to lose.

"The morning we could hear the shade of Miles was too lovely. And who should be standing in the middle of nowhere, and charming trees, wiggling worms, blowing his horn to his heart's content, but Al. Remember? What ever happened to him? You can ask that about almost everyone you know in New York. You can strike up a crazy, wonderful friendship, cry the common blues, have a ball, then bam!—never see the soul again in life. And at the time you were being friends, you truly were . . . I guess this is all we can have of friendship. That everlasting, over the 'Hi! neighbor' back-fence bit is just about so much schmaltz. New York can make you break out of your cocoon and make you want life for whatever it damned well is; and, at the same time, send you retreating into your hatched cocoon. Who in New York knows their next-door, across-the-hall neighbor? You can share the toilet and the bath with a ghost—as far as that goes. You would never know the difference. I had forgotten the Peeping Tom until I got started on Central Park. He, I am sure, will not forget us. We toyed with his standard thrill of looking from a removed spot at hot-time lovers. We were not too cruel to him, though. He got his cookie; but we made him get it by transmitting anticipation, suggestion. He made Peeping Toms out of us—too much. He looked pathetic playing with himself to the beat of nothing but laughter. Did we egg his rhythm on, or did he egg on the rhythm of our laughter? It was not so funny when he made it. He looked so hurt, surprised; as if he did not know whether to run down his little hill to thank us or slap us for giving him the new experience of doing it with his mind only. We should have charged him entertainment tax, or he us—one of the two.

"You and I have always gotten into trouble for laughing. Funny . . . We were absolutely wild, Jimson. We tried it anywhere. The portable lovers on the waterfront, propped against interstate trucks, on the roof, down the hall, up the steps, up high, down low, sand, grass, water, on chairs, floors, the bookcase. We typed out a natural hymn on your typewriter, remember? Too bad we did not have paper in the machine. Wonder what we were saying. The upside-down, nailed-to-the-heights fools. I was never afraid, Jimson, truly afraid, in those days. The time I could have been frightened to death was the night we were roaming up Eighth Avenue and happened on the Puerto Rican confirmation party. Little girls dressed in head-to-toe white give me the creeps. I am able to see generations from now, maybe the year two thousand and fifty-six. I see them hermetically sealed within ornate picture frames, sepia-toned, indistinct. I see a member of the family bending over a mantel, holding them up to the light, peering, trying his best to see, and asking 'Who was this? How do we relate?' When the fellow asked me to dance and you said 'Hell no,' I almost died. The look on his face. Then his buddies gathered around lending him a terrorizing proportion. Then when he fired off in fast, clipped Puerto Rican, and I didn't answer—damn . . . I am forever running into someone in New York who thinks that I am passing for Negro. Now, that is a joke. It is true that being anything in New York, even Negro, is a whole lot better than being a Puerto Rican in New York. We have never had it so good . . . Remember when they were being sprayed when they got off the planes? Spray all the planes or hang it up.

"With some of these phony-time white people, though, I assume the identity. They are so amusing when they approach you with nasal twangs of Spanish, broken English, and sign language. You can't help but freedom-fight, defend everybody's lot. I can understand their willingness to make me feel at ease, comfortable, and cozy by speaking in a familiar way; but what they fail to realize is that the air of condescension stinks. Falsetto. How do they know? What makes them assume that you cannot understand basic English? Color? Well, now really . . . And then to be insulted for passing, for denying my assumed birthplace; he had had too much party, I guess. On him, too, you put your old, one-pointed stare. It works. I am here talking to you now; and this certainly does not look like heaven. I was loving you so much in those days, Jimson. I could have split my soul wide open to show off love. Anything you wanted to do with me, for me, to me, would have been all right . . . made me holler YES. Yes, it was love. It had to be; otherwise, how can I reconcile all the mess of pain I have caused, the chaos? If I do not think it was love, I am finished. Lock me up as a mad, demon bitch. I don't know what it is or was not, but I never will go through that again—not to the degree that we played. Some like it hard, close to the core, snipping at the cord. Jimson, maybe I am merely saving myself by calling it by the name of love; defiling the most common want, that most God-realizing transformed state where each is both . . . Perhaps we never know until we have been in it, until there is a distance between us negating self, subjectivity. The sad commentary is that then we are out of it. In order that I am able to refute the warnings of my blasé company, and believe that I have not wasted time, energy, violated my flesh, not appeared the utter ass, I must make this love. Anyway, I know what it is not. I can sit here all night talking heaps of garbage and wasting breath. It is an action beyond words. Flagellum. Lovers intuit, laugh and cry, grunt and groan. Pulp magazines and S-rate movies give them heavy dialogue up until the last moment; then, in slow motion, a door closes, a leaf falls, rain drops, snow flakes, music plays. Stop me, please; I have become a syrupy fool talking like a wet-eyed lush; but I will say again that if ever I loved anybody, Jimson, you are it. That's a mighty anemic-sounding 'if'—hummmm?"

"You still cannot see me as anything other than a blundering idiot, can you? Why is it you think me incapable of remembering how we came together? I came and got you, remember? You see, Ideal, that is one major fault of yours. You think no one capable of nostalgia and retrospection but yourself."

"Jimson, you know that is not true, now . . ."

"It is definitely true, woman. You have come to believe that you are some sort of fairy of good wish and true love. That is just about so much nonsense. It makes me sick at the stomach. And it is my fault. I have convinced you that you are the angel of mercy, the abdication of all my pain, my inspiration and virgin soul. Well, I am sorry. You are a woman, a weak woman, a girl whose very physicality bespeaks child. I see no soft, warm lap of the world in you. I see no responsible person, no listening voice, no affirmation of myself, no gropings toward myself in you . . . You are a witch and a yoke. I will die from you. Drink up your drink and let's get the hell out of this damned place. Come on, now."

The tone had been set . . . The liquor and drinking too fast falsely intoxicated them. They would use this intoxication as a final cue.

"You are the cryingest woman I have ever seen. Must you always start those damned tears welling up in your eyes? Believe me, I am no longer impressed by the sight of them. You had me fooled. You could stand here and cry forever, but I am going back home—so are you. Come now, little girl."

"I hate you. I hate you, you black dog. You simpering, trifling phony of a man. You are nothing. You are the shame and mistake of all my life. To think that I walked out on a tender, loving, giving man for some sick beast such as you."

"Ha! you should talk. What happened to the burning confession of your heart? Excuse me, I forgot that a woman's heart lies between her thighs. The tale of woe you told . . . He was too weak for you, too dead, too lacking. He didn't question you, or fight you, weight you with the heaviness of his manhood. You wanted him simply because he was older and you were the simple schoolgirl trying to impress friends and a college boy who had taken your virginity. And don't you ever forget it; you wanted him, he did not want you. You are a fool, I tell you. You are a fool. You sit here and, just like a fool, understand and forgive a man who responded with the openness of a mollusk. Again, I say he never loved you; but you refuse to hear what I say, Ideal. Never forgive an insult. You should hate him, get up each morning, go to bed each night, preparing his downfall, your revenge. He does not deserve your sympathy, your concession. Why? For what? You allow a few faint whispers to change your mind, a few I-love-you's, a few forgive-me's to make everything all right. What did he promise or offer you—nothing! He practically had to be put in jail, threatened with torture, before he consented to marry you. Public opinion . . . And, even now, he thinks he is the bargain, the prize package, the innocent one. He asked, begged, that you piss in his face. What does that mean? Ablution? Guilt? Adoration for you?

Hell no! It means perversion, his inability to give, his inability to feel and realize you as a woman through his natural manhood. It takes some sick suppression to fascinate him. He made you not his wife, equal, or subject. He turned the emotion inward, upside down with an unwholesome idolatry. You became his master, his man. By begging you to enslave him, he became free to hate you, to renounce his virility. Mr. Ideal . . . You and your maudlin sentiment. I wish he would ask me to piss in his face; he would not have to beg. You will continue to be exploited by those less than you are so long as you allow your guilt-infested identification to beat you to death. In looking at him one time, you—no, not you— but someone with one degree of consciousness, an analytical adeptness, can readily perceive his masochism, his inadequacy for sensuousness, his lack of engendering a thrilling courtship and erotica with submission. He sees nothing as divine. In his self-indulgent indoctrination, he associates you with filth, uncleanliness. He really wishes a man to pour guts, essence, and masculinity upon that spot from which his own has escaped. He is only able to perceive the point-blank, the reality of a penny arcade, the neon-lit signposts. The damned eunuch, the passive whip. A good homosexual, and that is whom he truly desires, would laugh in his undynamic butt. They, too, seek a communicative exchange that negates difference, or, in their case, sameness, and creates the One. Even a money-hungry prostitute hates to see this kind of trick come calling. He means hard work, repulsion. His sort takes the last degree of quivering out of the flesh and leaves the love object cold, denuded, holding nothing but the thought—'What happened in his life? . . .' Don't give me that stuff about the love and comfort you had. You had a mirror, a rag on which to wipe your common, accumulated pain and lack. I should slap you down right here where you stand, you simple-minded whore."

The reeling couple stumbled and started, struggled and danced, across the street. New Yorkers hardly cared if they tore their respective brains out. Was love winning out? Absolutely no one was tearing through the streets proclaiming the virtues and divinity of love; or grabbing passers-by by the coat sleeve, fighting to explain the love in their hearts.

"Well, Mr. Jimson, I am not taking another step. I am going to stand right here, exactly where I am, and shout to the world the hell and much of love, yours and mine."

"Do it then! I could not care less. But you won't have me standing here to provide you with one forgotten line, one improvised gesture. Go to it, fool."

Jimson focused upon the gathering crowd, searching for that one look which would sanction his plight. Ideal overturned a wastebasket, mounted it, and looked every bit the girl who had played and climbed yellow hard-mud make-believe mountains. The old smells, the crawling creatures, the whirling colors, the shouts of rock bottom—exhuming themselves—flitted across her face supplying her with a multitude of excuses to really act a fool. The hysterical shrew was determined to play her part to the hilt.

"Yes, I am going to tell you, warn you. This is Ideal.

Look, take a good look. I am love gone wrong. I am that thing, whatever it is, which masquerades in the name of love. I am the mouth that seeks kisses for its own enjoyment—because it likes the liquid chasm. I am the woman who gives up nothing in the name of love, the woman who gives up what she lacks in order to gain what she does not know. I am all feeling, incapable of reason, mistaking kindness and sensuality for passion. With a warped vista and undisciplined flounderings, I relish the idea of marriage as living with God."

Ideal was past the point of embarrassment, of caring what people or "they" would say. Some figures in the crowd shook their heads and walked away. Some guessed that she was drunk, stoned, or carried away with histrionics.

"Yes . . . walk away if you like. I don't think you can hear what I am saying, anyhow. Ladies and gentlemen, I am most appreciative of those among you who choose to hear me out. I am not drunk. Of course, in the morning I will swear that my whisky instigated this little show."

She was reeking. Her hair was entangled in tears. Snot oozed from her nose and mouth. Her hand wiped and smeared the mess across her face. She glistened. Ranting was becoming her.

"Hey, Jimson, come back here and help me tell the story, the whole crying shame. Feed me fire while I tell them that I have discovered that you are not living the life that you so jealously constructed for yourself out of your solitary, confined imagination. You are not living the life that you fancy and dream about, that existence which you desire. You have cheapened the wish and image of whom you could become, how you could respond. You have made me understand your right and quest for liberty. Your complaints are valid. Vicariously, I can understand your plight. You say that you are a poet, that you must take the time and distance to write. I can understand your lack of interest for time-payment plans and twenty-year mortgages. There is no waft of an aromatic elixir in the smells of house-hold detergents and cooking grease. There is no conscious, aesthetic design in wet diapers draped across a radiator. The Master Mathematician eludes us upon a daily grocery list and a basic budget of our bare necessity. I can understand a Jimson hating his necessary tasks, pouting at the time clock, and wishing that he would quickly or magically become his style of man. I can see a Jimson glad to get out of a green-metal filing room—away from the simultaneous smack of typewriter keys and chewing gum. I can see you making a complete revolution through a revolving door, walking out and not knowing just where to go—and not wanting to be home. I have been imagining you in such a shining manner, walking with the rhythm and ferocity of the free wind. Get 'em, Jim . . . I have been seeing you living your poems, constructing yourself exactly as if you, alone, were willing it. I can see you talking love and soft words into some woman's eyes. I can hear your misgivings about me—your justifications. I can see her giving the cool detachment that fires your blood. I saw you living your life for the sake of your soul's expressions. I was scared to death that you did not love, but I could see why . . . You broke my heart, Jimson, because you were not doing those things at all. You counterfeited the man. You did not become the thought of which you are capable. You sold out. You sold out in the name of common gossip. The story took on the traits of the housewife's soap opera, the forsaken artist's true confession."

Some minor scuffle flared up along the periphery of the crowd. Jimson, tussling with one of the onlookers, swung and chopped down the space. "Let him pass," someone said, "that's his woman up there." Jimson had changed his ultimatum. He had come back to get Ideal before she killed herself acting the complete fool.

"Ideal, please get down off that thing and come home. I know you are leaving me. How many times have you threatened me with that dried-up statement? You have made me understand that I am not your man, that I stink, that I am black and ugly, that I do not satisfy you in any way. I agree with you. I am crap and we both know it. Come on now, Ideal, get down. Come on, so that I can be left alone. I admit that I am weak, seduced by the moon. You could have helped me, though. You could have waited for me. I am out and I know it. I would have come back . . . You say that I have robbed you of your identity, that I stole your fire. Could it not be that we exchanged these things between us? If I do not accept the gift that you bring, the gift remains with you. Right now, I am unable to say what it is that I have taken from you. I have not opened the gift of you. The whole experience is intact."

"Good God, Jimson, you make me sound like a souvenir. Perhaps we have unwrapped too much of ourselves. We let go the tinsel, the element of surprise. We courted the spirit of love. We wind up, publicly, the same old story. Shame on us, Jimson. Shame on you for not tracking down your beautiful, poetic dream. You have cheated your talent. You have deceived your concept of man and artist. You are seeking escape and sensuality, romance and sympathy. Are you serious? You seek someone who is frightened to death of you, someone who answers yes to everything. You seek someone who affirms your destruction, who assists you in affirming your negation and denial. You are a fool, Jimson, in the white man's world. No, no, no, you are not. You are a coward and a provincial who sees everything desired as against the law. You use your color as a crutch. You use sex as an excuse. You know nothing of what you so arrogantly preach. You preach a selfishly adopted but finely Buddhistic view of the universe. Your philosophy is impenetrable by such a fool as I. You are the fabulous man, the artist, the lover. You preach a convincing sermon of man's stalking the earth in search of his way. I believe in you, but you have convinced me to a degree that you have not convinced yourself . . ."

"It is your vanity, Ideal, that is torn asunder. It is the concept of your becoming that is changed. It is your dream of originality that is polluted. Only your vanity is violated. You wanted a man, a genius with a predetermined giant's will to be the one who hurt you. You have constructed the only man in life whom you would allow to deceive you and stop loving you. It is you who have set up the man and the conditions by which you could be slain and wronged. It is your vanity that is pricked, since it is by the traditional and prosaic theme that your history will be made. What makes you think that the man whom you are able to imagine would, naturally, respond to you? Could he lose himself in you? Can you answer to his call and need, Ideal?"

Jimson's questions droned on and on. Not one word received more emphasis than the other. The tone of his voice remained, always, the same. One had to prepare to hear each word and intonation. His voice was whispered, conscious of breath. Only when one had flattered him would his voice assume another aspect. It became fragile and gleeful, giggling and lisping with all the commotion of childhood.

Ideal looked down at Jimson from atop her trash-basket throne. She wanted to believe the man's words. She wanted to fall down upon the ground before him, hug him around his knees, bury her head in his thighs, beg him to forgive her; instead, she balanced her drunken form and posed, as if she were awaiting the descension of a miracle that would restore them unto grace. The exhausted crowd shuffled in the waiting, and moved in upon Jimson and Ideal, flinging the torn-to-pieces lovers together.

"Kiss and make up," someone in the crowd advised. Ideal pushed away from Jimson.

"No, no, people . . . this is not it, this is not the miracle I am waiting for. You have pushed us together. I am waiting for the spirit to do it for us, not you."

She grabbed one of the onlookers as if to make an example of him. On second thought, she swept the onlooker, who did not resemble spirituality, aside like a swatted fly. Jimson struggled with the crazy woman to take her home. She fought him with the backbone of a mad dog.

"I give up, Ideal. It is your show. Please have it."

"Take your hands off me, you contrived fake and risk. You bizarre, haunting, beautiful man . . . don't put your hands on me. Yes, I hate you. I learned to relish hatred in being with you. You are too clever for me, my love. You do not think for one moment that I believe that saccharine, compassionate look in your eyes, do you? It is a filthy lie. You pretend because you cannot accept the boy you really are. You are saddened only because your public sees you standing out here with your guard dropped. You are capable of great hatred. You hate with a power which demands that we give you our flesh, so that you may see our souls. You demand that the world empty its hard-earned purse, so that you may afford your aesthetic. You demand that the white man give you his identity, so that you may assume his color. What is your role, Jimson? Where is your place? What is your definite scheme for the universe? Whom will you blame, make wallow in the dust, kowtow to now?"

Tongue and mind were clapping, cutting through the night air with an eloquent clarity Ideal would be incapable of forming into language were it any other time, any other man . . . in life.

two

△

Climbing the stairs to the apartment choked the breath out of Ideal. As she arrived at her floor, the light burned out. Getting to the apartment door became a matter of instinct. She began feeling her way down the hall. If she could just get to the door, open it, and get inside, she vowed that never again would she drink another drop of sour wine. Her dizzy form bumped from one side of the wall to the other. She reached for a doorknob that was not there. She had walked this hall enough times to know its total structure . . . she thought. The misplaced doorknob knocked her to her knees. An objective view tickled alcoholic bubbles out of a high Ideal. Giggling, she crawled to her door. Oh, Lord . . . she could not find the key or the keyhole. She fumbled inside her purse. Each object had been chosen for its tactile quality; by the feel of its texture, she was able to determine its function. She made it, she was inside. The foolish accomplishment threw her back down on the floor. She lay there wallowing in giggles.

Jimson had not made a sound or a move. In total darkness, he sat smoking. Ideal caught a flicker of his cigarette's red light. The giggles slipped away into the stillness. Neither of them opened their mouths. What was this moment? Was he not going to dash her brains out, beat her half to death for having acted such a clown? Ideal could no longer control the pause. She gathered herself up out of the floor and started toward the closet to hang up her clothes.

No matter what shape she was in, Ideal practiced a disciplined orderliness clinging to the realm of hypercriticism. As she reached for a coat hanger, Jimson called her.

"Come in here, Ideal. I want to talk to you."

"I'll be there in a moment. I am trying to hang up my coat."

"Forget your coat and come to me right now, I say."

Ideal hung up the coat. Looking into the mirror, she felt repulsion for the image. She looked like hell. She refused to brush one hair, to wipe away one streak of smeared make-up. Arranging the chaotic view would have added another sentiment to her hysterical attitude.

"For goodness sake, turn on the light. Why are you sitting here in the dark?"

"I said that I want to talk to you, not look at you. Have you seen how you look? If you had any pride at all, you would not allow a soul to see you as you are."

"Jimson, you said you wanted to talk. I think that you still want to argue. I am prepared for either conversation."

"Sit down, woman. You make me sick with your petty sense of will power. You still do not know who I am. I would cut your logic to bits, woman; your confidence and intelligence would lie bleeding on the floor; but I do not want to hurt you, Ideal, I love you . . ."

"Well, you certainly have an unusual way of showing it, my friend."

"I want to talk, Ideal. If we do not consciously use this time, it will be too late for us. Your little street-corner scene has stripped you of your beautiful façade. You have revealed your weapons, denuded your pain. I see you now for what you are without pretension or mask. You have just murdered your glamour. If you will be quiet and listen to me, your virginity can renew itself. I do not hate you for your little scene. I heard your floundering in the hall. Again, your foolish intelligence saved you. What other lovers do you know, Ideal, who are able to survive this degree of pain?"

50

"Yes, Jimson, but we are practicing hatred. We have transcended that pain which is existent in the world, that evil condition which is the natural lot of mankind. We have gone a step further. We create it. We inflict each other with cruelty, not pain . . . You speak of my petty sense of will power. We have let go compassion. I think that your theory of the degree and quality of pain in relation to one's capacity to love is warped. I have known too many people with that sick sense of suffering. The 'more one suffers, the deeper the soul' movement. Did I ever tell you about Booker Shad, a true believer in that school? I knew him way back when. Sometimes, I feel personally responsible for his downfall by encouraging him to pack up and come to New York. He was a musician and had talent; that is, he sounded like soul back home. Anyway, he packed up, bought himself a bus ticket, and left for the big city with nothing but his hips and elbows, sixteen cents, and two cold waffles. He started hanging around musicians, talking that talk, and making himself seen, if not heard. He begged poor Charlie Parker to death to let him sit in.

"Well, anyway one night Yard was feeling good and sentimental and let dear old Booker sit in. Before they could get through the first number, Bird was giving him looks that let you know he could not believe it. After the tragic set, Bird told him, 'Look, kid, you do have some talent. You could develop into a real beautiful cat; but, man, you have got to study, to learn to love your instrument, to learn to read music. Those days are gone for jumping up on the stand and improvising your lungs out. If you really want to play, to become a pro, you will have to step on out, man, and take that step which will not leave you hung up in a room somewhere listening to yourself blow. The Apple is overrun with musicians —good and bad. Some nights, go up to Lewisohn Stadium and hear Bartók played to the open-air heights. It is a beautiful thing, my man. You have got soul, though, baby. I hear you. What you say your name is?'

"Well, Booker baby practically spit in Bird's eye, insulting him, accusing him of all sorts of outlandish plagiaristic practices. He had to be thrown out of the club. With horn in hand, he went back to his cubbyhole and dissected the advice. No, he did not go somewhere and study; instead he began accusing musicians of stealing his hummed refrains, snatching records off your player, smashing them on the floor, claiming that they—whoever 'they' are—stole his soul. He began shooting dope like a crazy man, trying to feel a deeper soul, a bigger ear for sound. Running through the classic junky gamut, he ended up either homeless or in and out of the Tombs. Every two-bit job he found, he lost for his craziness. He worked as a dishwasher, pulled a meat cleaver on the cook when the cook doubted his word regarding his genius. He used to come to our place and sit raging until he had to be wrapped in cold towels. For maybe a year, no one heard tell of him. Then one day he showed up announced by a boisterous crowd under our window. Perfect strangers he had begun insulting. Booker had on army fatigues, a fur cap—it was hot summer—the jacket to someone else's suit, and white boxer's shoes . . . the kind Kid Gavilan wore with style. We let him in, offered him a meal, but he could not keep the food on his stomach—it had been so long since he had eaten a full meal, or a scanty decent one. He started trying to tell us some off-the-wall story about Geronimo. It seems that he had definite, genealogical proof, through a dream he had one night in the Tombs, that he was the direct descendant of Geronimo. He revealed that he had been living in a cave in Central Park. With either a piece of coal or rock, Booker had cut tracks into his face so that there were unhealed scars running from his eyebrows to his goatee, from his mustache to his sideburns. It was unbelievable. He said he was training the hairs to grow in this design. He wanted to be hideous, repellent to people, to suffer, to create a deeper soul by people's derision and ostracism. All of a sudden, he leaped up, ran to the window, shouting below to passers-by, and singling people out, yelling down to them that they were shit. He ordered them to deport themselves, since the country rightfully belonged to him, the descendant of Geronimo. Beating on his tubercular-looking chest, he yelped like a movie Indian. Adam had to drag him away from the window. Booker fell to the floor, crawling like a snake, barking and snapping like a dog at me, and took a plug out of my ankle. Pleading to be kicked, to be put on a chain, to make him suffer; Booker had to be sent on his way, back to his cave. His war cry echoed back at the world, upstairs in the apartment, as he went down into the subway. The last I heard of Booker Shad, he had been confined by his mother. Something told him that he should go back home, I guess. Well, the something goofed. Booker got home, startled his old friends and neighbors with his New

York acquisition. He had left as a calm, serious, nice young man . . . Still not satisfied with his soul's depth, he went up and down the streets at, naturally, the oddest hours, blowing his horn. He was satisfied only when the police had been called. Calling them everything nasty, everything vile he could think of, except officer, Booker invited them to club him half to death. The knots on his head exhibited his soulful vastness. The bloody, terrible end came when Booker decided to rape his mother. He did. She called the law, signed the papers. Booker foamed at the mouth, screaming and choking on his own saliva, 'You are a traitor, my own mother, my dear mother. Can't you see you are wrong? These stupid, square asses will try to take away my soul, find out how I did it, so they can have soul; while they make me a white-jacketed machine just like them.' Charles Christopher Parker, Junior, never knew . . .

"It is our generation's expiatory beatification. You have gotten the notion in your head, Jimson, that you are the Giver of Light. Maybe, you are . . . but I am frightened when I think of the supremacy, megalomania, that such a concept demands. The Korean War and Japanese holidays confused your mind. You mastered on a furlough, a busman's holiday, the enigma of the East. Perhaps, you are the All-Seeing One. All of us have become instant Buddhas. We have put down our tribal-time religions. Good, the primal concept is too geographically encompassing. Everyone has become enlightened. A head full of esoteric, beautiful discipline is what you have, Jimson. It is a shame that you have warped it. You have made it a tool with which to beat down the world.

54

You present logical, airtight theories that I am unable to dispute: but my legendary, absurd intuition leads me to believe that it is wrong because it generates harm. You are exploiting the Divine for egotistical satisfaction. No one is able to refute you. As they say, 'No one is where you are . . .' It is a tragedy, Jimson. You claim the world is too thick-headed to receive your beauty. You have made yourself the Messiah, but whom will you lead? You leave the world totally unprepared to receive your message. You write beautiful poems, but no one is able to decipher their message. Sneering at them, you proclaim your disciples to be stupid. I don't know, Jimson, I simply don't know."

"If I am able to recall rightly, I said that I wanted to talk to you. I did not say that I wanted to hear your Jimson critique. No, Ideal, our little game is not over. It is far from being the end. If we must sit here the whole night long, we will. I am interested in the root provoking your thought. You will discover mine. One must never forgive an insult . . . Tonight, my love, I shall teach you how to perform, how to flagellate the mind—not the body. I will paralyze your mind, kill your faith, mutilate your hope. If after the vivisection, we are able to forgive, you will have the answer for which you wait."

The objects and furnishings embraced the breath of Jimson's plan. The wooden floorboards contracted, responded with a crack. The clock skipped a tick and muffled its alarm. Flowers in a delicate vase changed their color. Designs in the Persian carpet shifted their symbols. Ideal dropped her head and sank into the couch. Jimson propped up his feet and struck a match.

"But if you ever call me black dog, Ideal, I promise you that I will crush you to bits. For as long as I am able to recall, I have had that black business hammered into my head. Papa Boo, God bless his sweet soul, is my experienced definition of the pitiful huckster of the American Negro's paradoxical tragedy. His natural intelligence was involuntarily thwarted, so that he possessed only that intelligence which was the effect of the emulation of the white man. Alone, in his own thought or in the company of blood brothers, he was able to proudly reveal his historical condition, to appraise the good and evil of his living present; to reject and accept the governing forces, to laugh himself into hysterical tears tearing apart and reconstructing the system, to hang his head and bemoan his brother's lot. But when the maudlin sentiment was over and done with, when time said it was the hour to go and meet the man, his whole posture and attitude became victim of an unqualified metamorphosis. He became the pragmatist without a dogma, the creature who knew his assigned place, the numbered body who responded to a bureaucratic summons, the hieroglyphic recipient of so many farthings in return for so many hours. He was the virile stupidity that provided the impetus for his superiors to ride the crest.

"He fought for the rights of those who beat him into the dust, and upheld his sense of worth only in the company of his brothers. He was ready to inundate, to slay his own, if they were unable to perceive and sustain that which he himself had allowed to be usurped from him. Only from his brothers did he demand, only among

56

his brothers did he accuse and deny, or choose to act, at last, like a man . . . Papa Boo's ignorance was oppressive. He had been deathly frightened and, in turn, propagated the fright that consumed him. He was our gentleman boarder, who tipped along the block 'howdy-doing' everyone who gazed up from their activity to recognize the miserable old Uncle Tom. The moment he had passed by, the front-porch judges either laughed or sanctioned his slavery-time credo. All of them, however, bestowed an aristocratic halo upon his thick head; because he was the ten-dollar tither who had retired from the long, hard toil, suffering his lot unobtrusively, he lived to be rewarded with a paltry token from the great white father. I can see him now strutting through the street wearing the sleazy black suit of a defunct chauffeur. It shined in the seat with his self-appointed eminence. He drove master around for forty years, opened and shut car doors, tended the garden, stoked the furnace, cooked on the cook's day off, and assumed any other duties that anyone with an ounce of sense would have called free or donated labor. He referred to it as his sense of initiative . . . Papa Boo was the hypocritical flunky who could be trusted with master's life and household operations.

"He must have spent many a mile peeping in the rear-view mirror; eavesdropping on the man's conversations, yearning to become a partner in his world, wearing white gloves to dance the waltz, narcissistically rivaling his thought and action. The master died and left Papa Boo enough to pay my father exactly seven dollars a week for his temporal existence. That works out to approximately one dollar a day for forty years of emulation, puppetry, and scab labor. The inheritance rendered him too worthless to afford a proper linen collar to go with his suit. He fashioned a collar made of a hideous plastic material. He simply sponged away his putrid sweat and dirt. On top of the collar, he hung a huge, inherited golden cross. Yes, Papa Boo did a thorough job of convincing me that I was the Prince of Darkness, a shame before God, the ugliest child in the world. He slipped through our house excusing himself for his every unsaintly fart. He prayed over the table for twenty minutes and kept his eye on each mouthful you swallowed. The cheap white collar gave his neck the posture of a parasitic bird. The dinner table was a camouflaged battlefield on which he demonstrated the strategy that he had singly employed to win the First World War. The soup ladle always indicated himself. His honors and decorations varied each time he told the lie. The purpose invariably remained the same—liberty and justice for all, because the master had told him so . . . He signified all day long on the virtue of his belief, and waited until no one was around before beginning his persecuting discourse on my intense brown skin. He said that the Good Lord visited him in his searching moments and warned him that I had been issued from the devil to blaspheme my father. My mother, he vowed, was blinded at the first sight of me. I was the reason my people were kept down; anything that looked like me had to be kept back. He meditated upon a painting we had in the hall of the Virgin Mary and then marched off to confession to purge his foul mouth. I was a mere boy, Ideal, who had been taught to respect and never dispute my elders. I was the one to whom Papa Boo dreamed to issue orders from an upholstered back seat. He fulfilled his intention with his house-niggah consciousness. I became representative of the black dogma . . ."

Jimson sniggered. A cigarette ash flickered toward the floor.

"It is a lachrymose commentary that you resort to the myth, Ideal, and summon the black dog to berate me . . . Your tongue has more fluidity, wordiness. With all your intelligence and worldly heart, you still reveal your Bottom philosophy. Our generation will not transcend it. It is vague when I try to envision the generation that will be free. The situation contains such a fundamental, impossible nature. Through intellection, I know that without discrimination, there is no equality; yet I wonder just which generation will uncover and negate the eternal brainwash. Isolde of the fair hand—Isolde of the dark hand, the villain is dark, the savior is fair . . . Who will be relieved of this anxiety, fear, persecution, malevolence, this innate feeling of ineptitude? I know interracial couples of each possible combination who love and live happily as any other two people of like or disparate characteristics; but I have seen these same couples resort to all the familiar, brutally racist tactics whenever there was an unresolvable point. The majorities resorted to their innate sense of superiority, the minorities to their innate sense of contempt.

"Collectively, they trounced each other with the embedded exploitations of their equal myths and legends.

Well, as soon as I became old enough to question my elders and fasten my pants, I put it down. I shot myself through the tube in order to be absorbed in another change. I put them all down: the self-appointed leaders, the jack-leg preachers, the handkerchief heads, the country plus, the elite Negroes, the cats, the cars, all that chiaroscuro crap. One saves oneself. Not a damn soul attempted to alleviate my pain. What I become, I become because of what I think. My patience is exhausted bearing fragile tablets of unmanifested good. Harmony's name is low. I court the venomous grudge, the search for the X figure of possibility and dream. Nail them, I say, with their spikes of tradition and absurdity. We have broken through to the same people . . . What is the opposite of grudge, Ideal?"

Ideal had lost her three-dimensional being during the outpouring. She was melted into the couch's cushion. The sculptured eye of Kwan Yin, posing on the mantelpiece, peered at the flattened symbol Ideal had become —"Palliation for a Penitent Chimera." No response was equal to Jimson's declaration. Saying that she was sorry would give her the appearance of a well-disciplined child. Guffaws would crack the ceiling if she uttered, "I'll never say black dog again."

"Do you want me to open the window and let out some of this blasted smoke, or was that a nervous cough? We smoke too much."

Little Ideal could not breathe a word. Her brain was clutching each word that Jimson had just spoken. She was trying to affix relationships. The declaration had to contain Jimson's significance. Was this why he was

60

crestfallen when he discovered that she was not a well brought up Filipina? When they were introduced, Jimson assumed that she was Filipina or somebody from somewhere else. He defended his mistake by telling her he knew a girl who looked just like her. Was it because of Papa Boo that Jimson had gone as far as adopting a West Indian accent? Ideal was just as surprised to learn that he was an American Negro . . . Was any identity more qualitative than his natural one? It was a basic reaction. The American Negro learned that being black was synonymous with retardation. However, if one had the good fortune of having enjoyed a shorter boat ride from the old country—hurrah! Or if one wore majestic robes, golden rings, and spoke with the accented pronunciations of the wise men, the new world would display her democratic legends and constitutional prose one degree beyond the native-born's focal point. Papa Boo had told it as it is. If you be just a plain, old home-grown shade—forget it.

Jimson had his façade slashed to bewildered doubt, when he learned through the friend who introduced them that Ideal had said that he was the most beautiful man she had ever seen. She had to be foreign or a fool. This complimentary gossip had to be repeated face to face, mouth to ear. The friend's hearsay resolving Jimson's fibres, he schemed his perspective for a ceremonial capture devoid of saccharine sentiment, and customary sequence. He lay awake nights designing his conquest with an unholy selfishness. If the culmination took a moment, a morning, or a lifetime, he would wait. His wife would wait, too. Her whole life had been spent in

61

waiting to be removed from a hostile, uncatholic community of red, embossed, hermetic seals guaranteeing illegitimacy and the human error. She had come to Jimson encased within an avalanche of hard rock, in need of courage to sap her fragility. The unequal barter would lend itself to a predetermined compatibility, if Jimson would accept the hard-rock dowry while the newly nested bride reimbursed him with her inherited tolerance for toil. Their relationship, becoming invested with a weekly bank deposit, enabled them to make regular down payments on that trip across the river to Manhattan Isle. Jimson was the sure thing, the worthwhile investment who would finish school and take his professional place among the world of men who permit their tired brides to sit down, collect recipes, and knit afghans to drape over heavy lard bottoms and knees gnarled like old oaks.

Ideal, the splendid amusement, haunted his head with an aggressive phantom stalking his prey. For the capture, he would don the hair shirt, groom his beard until it scintillated with prismatic intention, wear trousers revealing the stud whom Ideal needed, choose shoes that accentuated his stealthy plan. Whenever the scheme was ready for the kill, Jimson would come calling on Ideal; and make her get up, stand up, call her husband away from his job, while he summoned his bride who had been waiting for the day and intuiting, daily, the unquiet secret in her man. Looking all of them dead in the eyes, the iconoclastic aggressor would announce aloud his desire from its inception to execution. The first intentional touch, to get the scheme moving toward killing day, would be to greet Ideal with an orange flower; catching her off guard, stunning her thanks with premature obeisance. Prayer would drift through the ether, pushing him toward the moment. The killing time would come.

The smoke, charging the discussion with pandemonium, threw Ideal into a coughing fit. Sneezing, she squeezed the breathless minutiae. Begging Jimson's pardon, she went off to the bedroom to expel the rest. She was the same wild woman who had come to the mirror a moment ago. The least she could do was comb her hair, wash her face. The floorboards squeaked as Jimson walked toward the room to find out what was detaining Ideal.

"I can understand your coughing fit and I excused your absence. You certainly could have the courtesy to let me know what you are doing, and what is taking you so long."

Instinct pushed Ideal behind the bamboo screen. Jimson could not imagine why she darted behind the screen as he approached. Naturally, he headed straight for the screen. What was she doing that she had to hide? He snatched her arm, dragging her out. He could see no trace of anything other than discarded clothes.

"Girl, have you any idea how you look? From the neck up, you are a sight. You have several sets of eyelids, one eyebrow, half a mouth, and your hair—it is electrified."

Their image shifted toward the mirror . . . the leash and the black dog. Jimson, aping their reflection, thrust Ideal upon the looking glass. The shock of the cold view contracted her flesh, releasing her hard against the aping man. The sun rays stiffened into blinkless arcs. Ideal had only wanted to wash her face . . .

Yes, she loved this glorious, wild, tragic man. Tickles and salty tears rumbled and swelled the time. The begrudging tongue began licking the eyes away, reshaping the mouth, contorting the brow. The leash was unfastened. The black dog was slipping the last word down the ear . . . transfigured. Nothing in the room took head; nothing responded to an argument's outcome. The answer, realizing this was not the moment for its coming, stretched out with fatigue, penetrated their limbs, yawned in turn, then spread for a spasm. The good answer blew a succulent sound down through the center of their common growl.

three

△

The skipped tick, regaining its time, incited Ideal to
choke its jubilant throat. On the mechanical beat, she
hit the cold floor. Instinctive resentment tumbled out
in space. The early-morning curse had resumed. She
grumbled, mumbled, demanding that the space reply.

65

Why was this her tradition? Jimson turned over, cursed the light and went back to sleep. Who had appointed her breadwinner? She snatched up her robe, cursed vehemently, and scuffed off to the bathroom.

If ever in life she was disarrayed by a clock again, she wanted the merciful Lord to take her away. Every miserable soul in the tenement was vowing the common ultimatum. And now, the water was cold. The man across the hall had gotten there first. She sat on the edge of the tub filling it with self-pitying tears. She was completely familiar with the get up, go to work, go home, go to sleep, get up and start it all over again routine. Jimson most definitely was not the messianic provider. He was lying in bed without a responsible bone in his body. His father had told her, though, the day she met him.

△

Ideal and Jimson had left the Village in order that sienna-lit suburbia, distance, and smoked leaves inaugurate their coming together. Jimson borrowed his father's flat for the ritual.

That morning of the meeting, sunlight aroused Ideal out of sleep. Jimson had risen early to shop for poetry, wine, and green grapes. Someone put a key in the door. Ideal assumed, of course, that it was Jimson. Before she could affix the night before or assemble a movie star's awakening composure, the someone unlocking the door bounded up the stairs. In the moment, Ideal recognized the lean salty bounder as Jimson's father. No one could have those eyes without consanguinity. They were pupil-less black and straight-set to the point of merging into a single eye capable of reading your mind with a cyclopian

66

perspective. The man continued charging upward oblivious of Ideal. What on earth did he want? Why was he rushing like the law hot on the trail of the wanted? Jimson had permission to use the flat. What was going on that Ideal needed to know?

Flabbergasted embarrassment, naïve defense, slackened the father's advance when he reached the landing. Ideal, the crumbling stone temple guard, armed only with dare, questioned the father in an amateur tone of theatrical affront. "And who might you be?"

The father, simultaneously, demanded the same statement of identity. He did not know Ideal and, further, he did not give a damn. He knew, however, that his son had come to him to borrow the flat, solely to take hold of his direction and discover his utility in an evolving world. The landlady had telephoned the father to report that a big-eyed girl had moved in bag and baggage. The girl and his son kept her awake by laughing off and on all the night long. During their convulsions, she could find no peace until sunup. The flat was contracted to be let to a quiet, single gentleman who tipped his hat, walked meekly, smoked nothing, practiced temperance, feared God, and straightened the lace doilies when his only surviving relative departed the parlor on Sunday afternoons.

Ideal fumbled for apologies that had lost their effect. There was no need to bear the brunt standing out in the hall. The father instructed Ideal to be still and just listen. He loved his son until the tears reddened his soft-talking eyes. He was a good boy, but an uncommon boy. His scholastic record reimbursed his dear mother's sacrifice. With Sagittarian style, he could ride anything from an Apaloosa to a rocking horse. He took his mark, ran track, and received the athlete's triumphant cup —his flying feet never did touch the ground. He was the hero's child, the fiery son who beat a dog to death for barking at colorless butterflies. In backyard grasses, yanking up weeds that obeyed with flowers, he had read books until his imagination passed out. Once, he wrote from Korea asking for an advance with which to buy a horse—a house—he never did do a good job of writing plainly . . .

"Yes, I love my boy, little girl; but in my heart I know Jimson is a dreamer. And I accept the full blame for what he has become. I raised him to be a gentleman, an esquire. He had tennis lessons, piano lessons, horse-back riding, anything he thought he wanted. He has had his own automobile since he was fourteen—a thorough-bred pony at seven. All his clothes came from the finest stores in New York. And he will tell you how I used to whack his knuckles until he learned to master a knife and fork. He can dine in the company of kings . . . Maybe it was wrong, because I do not have a dime to leave him but, like all parents, I wanted the best for my boy. I knew what it was to be poor and hungry, walking miles down a red clay road to school, living in a clapboard shack, hearing my mamma and poppa pray-ing to the Lord to relieve them and give them the strength to move on. I know what it is to live behind the sun . . . I swore that no child of mine would ever know that life or hold his hat in his hand before a living soul; and that he would be better off than everyone I knew, and able to match wits with all that I did not know. I hate a coward, a weak thing—especially a black one. I do not know what Jimson is going to make of himself. I wish he would go back to school and become a lawyer or something. At least, he would have a stick to fight with. He would have security. No one could take it away from him. Goodness knows that he has a gift to reason and squabble . . . That poetry and art business he has in his head will not bring him a penny. It will drive him crazy, though."

Father was elegantly dressed in the East Coast look. He wore tailored mohair, a cashmere coat, fine English brogues, an exquisitely mounted sapphire. He pointed out, on the street below, a dazzling convertible car. Everything that he owned now was his hard-earned reality-stamped paid-in-cash. Once upon his dandy time he had fallen in love with a girl from the Midwest, a doctor's daughter. In discordant unison, his family and her family agreed that they were of different worlds; that she needed the professional, educated man, one who could relate to her upbringing. Father would have brought her down in the eyes of her society. What was he? Who was his family? What was his earning power? What had they done for the pride of the race? By the time he could impress her people and respectable friends, it would be too late—out of mind.

"It is a dirty shame when our own people believe that mess that has been pushed down our throats. We really believe that white is right. I let him have this place to give him time to face life squarely. I know something is bothering him. It is going to take time for my boy—time and money. He cannot give you what I can tell that you are accustomed to and deserve. You are the picture of that lost gal of mine, as sure as you are sitting here. I do not even know your name, baby; but I know my boy. Please go on home and just pretend that Jimson never passed you by, that this is not you at all . . ."

△

The water was hot. It was about time. Ideal stepped into the tub and cursed human hair stuck to the soap. No, this was not the manner in which she chose to live her life. She had been spectator to the condition in another life. An incarnate Adam had brought Ideal to New York on a cold morning—an aeon ago. With palette and dance slippers in hand, they had arrived in search of the classic dream. Having outgrown the province, they wanted the big city and all that it afforded the dreamer, the spectator, the inoculated soul. They had tiptoed through each square inch of hometown's museum, borrowed the world's literature from its library, attended visiting artists' one-night concerts. They were impatient to court the dynamic awe. New York was where they had to be, if they wanted to realize the life, learn their crafts.

Adam and Ideal had not run from blatant Jim Crow, the heinous lowland, opportunity's lack. The good life had existed in a material degree far beyond hometown's average family. Why they were not realizing their aspirations was an indistinguishable factor; a factor fathomed, but elusive of finger-pointing blame. Hometown was an industrial town, the greatest in the world, for its chronic generation of the capitalistic system, the statistical achievement of the Negro as both an indisputable buying and ballot-box power, and the representation of skilled and unskilled workers as human dignity's collective force. In such an environment, concrete needs could be nourished, material visions dispersed. But . . . the people's hope and ultimate goal nestled afloat in the caul. The achievement of total uncontested involvement within the American society, of which they were natural-born citizens, was yet a minus symbol upon statistical charts. Hometown could parade before posterity's eyes a glorious star-spangled banner of first Negroes to be elected, appointed, promoted, and hired in those niches heretofore reserved and deemed only suitable for the Caucasian heart. Ambition was meted out to a qualitative esoteric. The people, seeking neither favoritism nor pity, had endured the scourge of slavery, outrage, injustice, segregation, and unequal opportunity in each gasping breath intrinsic to survival. That they had participated in the new world's struggles, civil and world wars, given their integrity and sweat to projects for which their return was in the form of reimbursement equivalent to free and donated labor could not now be negated and determined as futile effort. Time had become perceptible. Hometown was readying for the walk armed with moral and soul force as its swinging weapon. Ideal and Adam were out of step. It was best that they move on, discover some form by which their intangible fortress could be utilized.

Adam and Ideal were free to ramble over hometown, partake of its proffered programs, grass-roots politics, public events. Invitations were freely advertised. They could

71

not, though, tire of the unilateral focus upon feathering the rich's pockets and gerrymander the system. They could not find fault with fifth-rate housing and summon a van to cart them away. The Anglo-Saxons, Irish, Polish, Italians, and Jews enjoyed this privileged consecutive order of seniority. They could not prosecute quiescent de facto segregation. They could not burn their textbooks and demand that their tax dollars be refunded or purchase supplemented educations. They would be defeating themselves to insist that token representation of blacks be dismissed as a farcical good deed. Citizens' improvement associations would have railroaded them out of town had they attempted through their amateur media to express resentment for hometown. Adam would have been scraped from his canvas, Ideal frozen in her interpretive rhythm. The time had not come in hometown to indulge, patronize the creative will. Hometown was not subsidizing sloths, idlers, and ne'er-do-wells. Industry demanded a contributive, definite energy from black and white. Propagation of the system was not fueled by abstract elements. What could Adam and Ideal produce that was black and white? Dollars were green that would bring forth the caravan to the promised land.

The couple looked like tadpole-eyed foundlings when they got off the timeworn train with several paper suitcases, forty dollars, no regrets, and the unpackageable parcel . . . hope. Adam and Ideal could endure anything. Success would be a chronological matter . . . They had kissed goodbye the thermostat, the regular meal, the milkman, the green grass, the colored papers, the installment plan. It was the typical embarkation, the young people's deluded dream infused with unsubstantial bugbears and a fugitive tourist's gazetteer, which mapped out the city as the steel-pillared Sodom, the blindfolded rental agent, the as-it-ought-to-be mecca, the equitable employer, the philanthropic grocer, the armless bill collector, the color-blind registrars of local and private institutions of national manufactured learning. Ideal and Adam had heard the propagandistic bark of "Come as you are—Go where you like—Leave when you must . . . the Big City's a ball for one and all." They believed that hometown was forging automatons, while the big city was riveting aspirations into sperms of individuals.

Hope is hard rock for carpenters and fools.

Their new home was transformed into an atelier, a chapel, a hostelry, a cafeteria for a world of next-door neighbors who had shut their hometown's door. In a dreadfully small apartment, Adam and Ideal took up the game. They closed out the compressed world of racism and materialism. Citizens, equal in their pain and quest, knocked on their door looking for the way out. Ideal fed them from a kitchen that was so small that, while she cooked, her toes stuck under the kitchen sink, her behind in the living room. The place had two windows overlooking the brickside of a theater. In order that ventilation blow across the room, it was necessary to keep the front door open. Adam dyed a bedsheet, hung it from the ceiling, and continued paying the landlord for the price of one. They were in New York and that, after all, was the purpose. The boys call it "Dues

City." One must pay many dues to one's temperament and desires in order to maintain the solicitous change and kaleidoscopic pulse which is the "Apple."

△

Ideal pulled out the stopper. The bubbly water drained. Her cursing mood refused to budge. She slammed the door and hoped that the noise would shake the stew out of the sleeping Jimson.

"Get up, niggah! Who the hell do I look like—your mother or your rich patron?"

Jimson raised his head, lowered it, recognizing that it was only Ideal going through her morning monologue.

"I have had just about all that I plan to take off of you, Mister. Get up now and amount to something. And don't give me that nonsense about how difficult it is to find a job in New York equal to your undiscovered dignity. It's showtime! Roll out! Get yourself together. I do not plan to support any man but my own son; and right now, I do not have one. Matriarchy is superseded by the giant's will. You sit around here crying the blues about the fate of the colored man, the historical apronstrings to which he has been tied, the subservient position you occupy in life. You've got a lot of nerve. Do you think you will create your grace and virility lying around on your haunches? What makes you think that I am strong enough to bend without breaking, to face the man day in and day out? The shackle is gone from my leg, too."

Ideal had resumed the search for the missing miracle. Jimson was stirring now.

"I am looking for a man, my friend. What is it you represent?"

"Give me time to open my mouth, woman. You had better move on before you make the boss man angry with your disregard for arriving on time. I have taught you one lesson well. One saves oneself. I am not responsible for you or to you. I have taught you to take care of yourself. I am a poet and I will persist in living the existence conducive to the calling. What do you wish that I do? Push a truck through the garment center? My manhood dwells within my mind, not my muscles. Of course, there is always Nedick's, civil service, and skilled-trade schools. I could take up a trade at night while you sleep . . . butchering, maybe. I am a man, Ideal, and don't you forget it. I am not a bourgeois, however. I left the world of honest labor long before I heard of you. It is not my intention to make a profession out of having someone tell me what to do—particularly the white man or you."

"Yes, sweetheart, I know; you are the poet laureate of Greenwich Village. Let me get myself out of here before I lose my mind. I like the habit of eating. If we receive another eviction from Frankenstein, we will have enough to wallpaper this whole damned apartment. Goodbye, fool."

The tears welled in her eyes again. Jimson had won this round, too. She started down the endless flight of stairs. She hit the pavement, rounded the corner, put on her sunglasses to hide her puffy eyes. The characters had changed names and personalities, but the scene was unaltered. Adam had heard the initial tirade. He had retorted with an identical rationality. Her eyes were too wet to see beyond contradictions. Her father and many fathers had worked the honest day all their lives.

75

Their dignity was still intact, their minds balanced, their accomplishments respected. She had seen her first giant leading the people in the little corner church. She knew the history of the black man's struggle, idolized the leaders and sojourners. The artist's hard time she knew by heart. The same or a worse fate had been their obstacle. Was dignity a tangible asset of which one could be robbed? Was determination out of step with dream? Resignation was for the weak-hearted, those whose patience was exhausted.

Ideal stopped under her favorite ginkgo tree. Taking in its sublimity acted as a catalyst. She must be collected before the workday began. Ecstasy had no elusive cause. It produced its magic brazenly. Gimmick was reserved for the schemer. Jimson tormented her with flowers, anointed her confidence with the words of Jesus Christ, and scented her convictions with his unctuous creed until her petals slid down one by one. "You are withered, Ideal. You flowered before our time."

If she were not careful, the tears would come back. She moved up Fifth Avenue with the speed of the happiest woman on earth. Ideal could not afford to be late another morning. Jimson was right. Ideal must have flowered in another incarnation. The seed had sprouted a fallow pistil. Her sole contribution had been in nourishing the homeless visitors. Going back and forth to work was no grand achievement. She could have remained in hometown for that task. The reward would have been more beneficial. The standard of living for the many, surely, was higher. She would have enjoyed good plumbing, central heating, and the prospect of saving a few dollars from her meager salary. Soul food would have been her daily fare. Her hips would have been hefty, her skin clear. She could have cried the blues in search of the twinkling bread and peered at television while her eyelids drooped. Environment would have afforded her the arrogance and strength of the people. Color would have transformed her into a freedom-fighting spirit. Her complaining tongue would have been translated into the people's complaints and needs. Practicality would have served her fruitfully. The mirror would have reflected a black Ideal walking to freedom in the name of right. Becoming somebody would have been the challenge. Rise up! would have been the call. She would have courted the giant's will. She would have seen him laughing in a dark green suit. She would have told him, "I don't know you too well, sweet man, but please pocket the stunted orange flower"—like the sun in her room—"that I picked one night on the Vegas strip."

They would have been high and laughing . . . an entourage of celebrates, daffy girls, silken scarves, a belching Jaguar car, a man who sang, a man who prize-fought, a man who preached what is. They would have interrupted their single mood just long enough for Ideal to fish from forbidden grasses the orange flower; that is, if she had remained in hometown. The flower would have been love's gesticulation.

Come, leave whatever it is that you must. Travel, Ideal, with us to wherever it is you wish that you were; rather than hurrying up Fifth Avenue to beat a clock that will always be exactly where you left it. For now, let it be Washington, D.C. That town lies so uncomfortably beyond U.S. this or that . . . red dust roads, bad coffee, sinusitisly miserable air-conditioning, dirty toilets, greasy doors that used to bear signs which were the only available signs out of which some were able to create eminence for themselves: WHITE—COLORED. She would have traveled past Hagerstown—Town of Hager —no matter what the intonation or rhythm given the sounds, it still all came out, "Ladies and Gentlemen, you ain't missed a thing in this life you are living now, if you never visit or revisit this here town again. I mean this now."

Ideal would have walked to freedom up and down the land, if she had never left hometown. When she would have arrived at her hotel after the walk, crazy boys with frothy mouths and bearded chins would have scaled the walls and crawled the floors, vomiting time after time their total hurt and the sound of no. White men would have remained in their seats and cried apologies of, "It's not my fault." Whisky would have poured, perfumes would have reeked, guests would have come, guests would have gone. Telephones would have rung our two boys—the frothy and the bearded ones who could not consume their quickly coming convulsions. Next, they would have been up against the wall. Next, they would have been oozing snotty tears over the inabilities of those who could not or would not love them . . . Ideal would have shouted, "Reserve for us, quick! anything that will shuttle reality into another city and out of this town. Goodbye their Washington . . . another time, please."

78

An abbreviation would have best suited her next stop. The city would have been Chicago—instead of New York. The state was Ill. South Parkway and the Southside were locations within the recessed thoughts of Ideal's scurrying-to-work mind. Her will had rendered romantic such places a long time ago. At age fifteen, she had come to believe that she was, at last, grown. The monied possibility of her purse converted South Parkway, the Southside, into places one must visit in a lifetime. Roadside billboards heard her Hello. Lake Shore Drive heard her Goodbye. No good, so long. She would be back shortly.

When Good God answered the prayers of an Ideal who would have lain in a little hotel room that featured spotty wallpaper, and a connecting bath with voices of those who had chosen to gargle and party, He would have blessed firmly with a form that assumed the shape of an expeditious bird. The bird would have shot those who had prayed off into the night. Jetting along, dear Chicago, Ill., you would have become along the horizon of Ideal's vision; shots and sparkles, bubbles of alcoholic colors. Yes! she would have been looking good whilst getting gone. Quite frankly, Ideal fancied a whole scale of breath and tone that would have saved her had she never left hometown.

four

△

Dust is dizzied in New York. People are powdered with an opaque, gritty haze. Trespassing their separate existences, they fructify in a nomadic flux. Spawning in pigment is not where the soul lies. Ideal thought about the Moarbedan point in which Jimson indicated that a

80

woman's soul lay. He had come to determine its divine place in woman but not yet within himself. Attainment would be within our grasp, if we were able to nurture desires through their origin, exploitation and exile; but the greedy hog harbors within us digesting desire, and squealing with constant dissatisfaction. Someone in the crowd smelled like a pig, a big fat swine-natured slob.

"Excuse me, please." Ideal, bumping into a nomad, fell back into the swing of the fast-moving crowd. Home-towners had warned her about the swiftness of New York. They swore the town was callous, heartless, much too fast. "A wonderful place to visit, but not to live." One must be wholly aggressive and prepared to grovel for the daily bread. The people had no manners, and would knock you down as readily as they would pick you up.

A fire engine screeched. Ideal still became terrified by the engine's siren. Surviving planks and burning people enlarged the confined pupil of her soul's eye. Perception would not allow the memory of a hell-burning eternity to lie quiescent in the pit of her stomach. The sound was nauseous. She passed a delicatessen. The sticky cakes looked good, including the one on which a fly flitted. Insects, people, flowers, plants, animals on leashes, tanked fish, condemned fowl . . . everything stays hungry in New York.

Fingering her package of cigarettes, she estimated the remaining number. Without having to tear off the top of the package, allowing the cigarettes to become stale, she had learned to count the package's contents and thereby ration the weed out to herself. The quantity decided how her last cent would be squandered. Cigarettes won out, of course. Stepping on the sidewalk a moment beyond the reverberating thud, Ideal began playing a motionless hopscotch. "First my will, then your will. Now it's it. Walking over our gritty-eyed missions is foul play. Intrusion is not the way."

The corner flattened itself for the onslaught of shoe soles. Several blocks ahead Ideal could see neon lights blazoning TAKE OUT—HOME COOKING. The lights blinked downstairs under the office in which she worked and speckled the office walls with an uneatable, greasy invitation. A dingy subway kiosk swallowed down some of the fast-moving people. The decomposition giving Ideal's red suede shoes the opportunity to shine caught the attention of a lascivious look until a popcorn's stand immaculate white front raised up and stole the show. The owner prided himself on scrubbing the storefront each day the Lord gave him the strength to lift his arm. A fruit juice, hotdog stand smelled with its stench of poor-grade beef, rancid juice, strewn napkins, squashed cigarette butts. Its funky owner coughed over his products and hawked publicly on the floor.

Florence, the proprietress of a ladies' personal garments shop, posting herself in front of her shop, sat on a straight chair she had borrowed from the beergarden next door. Florence was determined to guard her best trick, her one reward from the game of life. The light was changing to green. Ideal ran to catch it. She crossed the corner, hopped the curb, ran another step or two—EMPLOYEES ONLY. Yes, it was showtime again. Time to enter the career girl role, read the Dear Sir script, pretend to be efficient, upstage competitors, and sing choruses of "pay you back on pay day." On her right in the building's lobby was a door leading to a dentist's office. Laughing gas opened her nose. On the left two swinging doors led to a Gypsy Tea Kettle. The kettle steamed up the lobby with incense and moldy tea leaves that had drunk up their sense of prediction. Little ladies in white gloves, looking as if they carried neatly folded black lace headpieces in patent ordered bags, frequented the Tea Kettle during those hours in which their fellow sisters sprinkled holy water and knelt in prayer. Their proper-fitting hats bordered expressions shameful of forgivable sins and devilish proddings to outstep tepid faiths, prescribed practices. The urge to prophesy futures could be quenched by swallowing down a cup of tea.

The street's reek, the popcorn's burnt butter substitute, the beer's impotent hops, the tropical, slopical juice, the stained red hots, the subways' lime dankness, the bus's exhaustion, fused with the laughing-gassed future. The rusting, squeaking elevator descended. Oiling its hinges would slick down its weariness, perhaps. The gates unfolded Ideal a step closer to beating the clock.

"Damn, let me disentangle myself out of this early-morning walk, so that I am better able to meet the man . . ."

Ideal assumed her place among the fixtures for another eight hours. The business to be processed lay before her. The man opened the door, glanced at Ideal, rechecked his wrist watch. Ideal and the watch were synchronous. Noticing her puffy eyes, he switched on the light. The inspection and the unspoken order were discharged. He said not a word and closed the door. His

83

expectation remained to charge Ideal with the will to produce or get out. The business world had no time for hysterical women with mutinous minds. Ideal picked up a manila folder. She unfolded a memorandum for unclaimed hemp. The light flashed on the telephone. The man would sign a requisition for a new desk lamp. She thanked him for his humane observation and returned to the file folder to reassure his trust. The work was not complex. Trafficking hemp and seaports transported daydreams into such freewheeling supposition.

Nothing Ideal had done in the world of wages and hours had been an insult or an unthinkable task. She would remember to bring this point to Jimson. She had plainly written reams of applications, impressed a recurrent conglomeration of interviewers with the obvious reason why she sought employment, and how her past experience qualified her to fit in well. The interviewers noticed each fidget she fought and wrote in neat handwriting upon the application's corner, Yes—No—Consider—Unsuitable (too much imagination)—Negro. She had been ushered through many office doors, remained a moment or for a while, donated for wedding gifts and get-well cards, worked overtime and undertime, executing duties that seemed vital or effete. Common sense revealed the meaningfulness and paper-clipped the function to the whole.

Ideal looked for some point in the office to transfix her. Contemplating an anemone's center would not do it. The pistil was indigo and opened to be touched. She fingered it. It was repellent, feeling like fur and flesh wrapped around a bone. Some object had to be prepared to transport her. Which one was it? Ideal had no need to provoke additional anxiety. Doing the work she was paid to do would relieve her; but the acknowledgment was immune from caprice.

She scheduled the duty to be concluded by lunch. The remaining hours of the day would be spent thinking about the duties to be concluded by tomorrow's lunch hour. She resumed her hunt for the workaday talisman. The object must take her out of mind, gag the apprehensions that were being voiced aloud. She was worn out with self-indulgence, cutting to shreds the flaccid fibers of her confidence, and analyzing everything and everyone as unattainable or impotent. The anemone was not concerned with transmutation. Jimson did not possess the will to witness and transfer the charm. He preached that one must save oneself. His plea was, "Take me away." The invocation was misanthropic, self-seeking. He magnified her frenzy with dissonant snores. Ideal dismissed the charm. Unclaimed hemp prevailed.

△

Luis Pagan entered the office. The predetermined "Good day! How are you?" dialogue was exchanged. Ideal could scream out loud to cut loose tradition and greet intrusion with spontaneity and words devoid of antecedent arrangements. What was said would evolve from a primordial tongue. Intuition spawned no offense. Omitting Hello—How-are-you wrought no contempt or gaucheness. Could not the greeted hear beyond the accustomed phrase?

Puffy eyes and the unopened folder exposed any lie

she might concoct about how fine she was feeling. Luis had brought her the daily cup of coffee. Ideal invented a reason to induce him to walk the length of the office. Luis was the Spanish dancer in exquisite leather boots, tight-bottom britches, and Sulka silk shirts. The walk strung out puritans, diverted attention, bulged browsing eyes, soothed aching joints, and switched on lights. He had it working . . . Ideal could not get enough of gazing at the man. She created unmanifested acts that remained in the realm of IF. Consummation was singularly reserved for the giant. Luis was the beautiful sight to expect each morning, the vision to fancy, the respondent ear. Here was the talisman. If the amulet were rubbed, the charm would split. Ideal had no desire to touch the swaggering man with the citrus smell. Seduction rested in supposition. Jimson would have killed her or perceived the submission. It was enough to tease with accidental brushes, focused surmisals, scents of edible breath.

She had learned to predict the outcome; having outplayed experimentation, the understood stare, hopping in and out of beds, feeling less than she uncovered. Proposals contained an equal wish, and charged nymphs, prudes, satyrs, and eunuchs with the possibility of uncovering the giant between the sheets. She was fed up with affirmations of her good looks, the feelings she excited. Her man stayed aroused, hammered down her soul, and slept days while she worked. Nothing was forcing the miraculous change. The wish was superior to the act, the outcome inferior to the proposal.

Jimson had struck Ideal's chord when they met denouncing Saturday night fucking, the nighttime creepers, the infantile adulterers. Both had gasped at his spontaneous, critical outburst. In the moment, they perceived their common past. On his wedding night, Jimson had coveted another woman on the rooftop directly over his new wife's head. The violated woman passed out when he whispered in her ear the name of another he would have desired instead. Jimson had seduced the hideous, the luscious, the imbeciles, the brains. He had become saturated and softened looking for the woman that would hang him, crucify him, gas him, in the name of love and death. He had mastered the trick, telling the nondescript they were beautiful, the beautiful they were brilliant. Prancing across rooms in a suit of flesh, Jimson jumped up on top of chairs, whipped out a yard long of plumage, and bowed to be begged with heart-fluttering approbations. He knew that his rightful calling was to be a pretty pimp dressed in camelskin shoes. However, a poor girl, who had not a dime, revealed his calling all over school. The pimp was expelled at ten years old.

Ideal could not rectify her errors and acts with the adoption of a Christly attitude. She had stamped the old law beneath the covers, and sucked the blood out of love, truth, beauty. She felt repugnance, wished to cloak that which might disgust. She waylaid Luis with the latest word, the enigmatic doctrine. Ideal clothed herself with a virtuous modesty, postured as a novitiate renouncing the world. Unshrouding her life would offend the man. Disillusion would slap his face. It was better that nothing bothered nothing. She had bathed in showers of sachet confetti, shivered on satin sheets, listened to the groove, ground the beau hog, tightened on the jerk, cursed the cause.

Luis displayed the gentle heart, the compassionate hand that patted the shoulder with "I understand." Ideal could talk freely, shift in her chair, uncross her legs, tuck in her blouse, wet her lips, without feeling as if she were being eyed through an open fly. There was no defensive pretension of headaches, flatulence, unsolvable problems. Luis allowed her the freedom to be another self. Desire was not stalking the fleshly land.

It was obvious that she was living with a man. She hurried to work and exited with precaution. When she took her lunch with Luis, Ideal sat facing the door, watching the window. As they walked the street, she looked back, advanced or withdrew, if co-workers appeared. Ideal never spoke a word of Jimson, but he was imprinted all over her. If the telephone rang, she turned aside, spoke low, made an excuse for being away from her desk during the time that it took to go below, dash across the street to a male figure, open her purse and shake his hand. Perpetually, she returned with the smileless smile. Luis learned to avoid her company when this move was made. He knew though . . .

His wife was the freakish blond with a passionate streak for charge accounts, leather-scented perfume, country tweed, and sleeping late with dark-skinned men. Luis had danced his silver taps off preserving the woman who castrated him. For Luis to accept Ideal's introduction to the hairsplitting love of perfection was an abrupt but facile transition. Self-denial would eradicate the sentient trappings. The divine play, the pause, the metaphysical content of the dancer's world was brutally usurped by the handful of "give me and you owe me this . . ." Coffee and toasted bagels received many a salty tear, many a forlorn question beginning with, "Remember when you were dancing, did you feel?"

Ideal had felt the problematic mood that rides the dancer's back as an unrelenting tension refusing to succumb to mental gymnastics and wishful thinking. The will to achieve took on a maniacal, dictatorial quality localizing itself as a gossamer covering and fitting tightly over the dancer's spine. Sleep, suspended from gigantic balls and chains, swung faster and faster. Space and Ideal disintegrated into infinite molecules. Learning the art form left her crying and cursing, vowing to get the technique, to make it second nature. She despised the form in the mirror that was not strutting a guinea-hen dancer. Day was filled with counted breaths and footsteps, initial incantation, final blasphemy. Night was a dream world with heretic writhing with the giddyup of acetylene spurs. The horse pranced combinations of embryonic, ethereal movements. The moody rider was challenging mercilessly toward the mark for the prize of the high calling . . .

"You are merely finding yourself as a dancer," the master consoled. "You are fortunate, blessed to be finding it so soon; some never find it at all."

Through the breath, the dancer comprehends all, nothing, physical perfection. Fantasies are negated as the body's center is intuited. The dancer dances and gives it all away—back to the center from which it begins. The mind-mirrored sensation of gesture exhausts intellection and leaves no attachment other than kinesthetic response, Holy Communion. Delirium resides in being calm with grace.

Through the needle's eye, on fire with goodness, Ideal was being transformed to the ultimate puppet; simultaneously dancing to herself, out of herself.

Presence was apprehended and directed always toward the need of at-one-with the Spirit. The magic moment descended; the body in the mirror was transformed. Sleep, engulfed in a sulphur haze, elevated desire, applauded accomplishment, engendered dream with a new craving. Who would hear her wordless affirmations, share the ecstasy, identify with the experience? Adam had lain next to her during those student days, refreshing his soul, gathering strength to get up the next day to earn the tuition that would keep Ideal afloat in the radiant haze. If the Lord would just send her down the black prince . . . If the voice would come whispering complete acknowledgment, assuaging the fury with concepts beyond those that Ideal offered; she would embrace the prince, tease, love him with the delightful instrument she had become. Prayer must manifest itself as a black giant seducing her out of herself, expounding deep-tone, quixotic conversation.

△

Luis, enticed by the reminiscent garblings, nodded "Yes, I remember. I know." Because of the hunger for a godlike ecstasy, of doing all in the light of that end, the two allowed coffee to get cold, the job to go to perdition. In love's death rattle, victims clutch the unlikely straw, the failing light—as panic moves them toward the living end.

The irrational rescue is as real, as comforting, and throws them off the wheel, frees them from meandering activities, washes off the cosmetic.

On those evenings which Ideal knew there would be no trace of Jimson, she and Luis rented a by-the-hour dance studio. The dance, inducing a motor narcotic, sent them spiraling to their respective corners to resist and release on a breath; until the mind went empty, the body entranced. They practiced the dressing-room ritual for the what-that-is-asunder with the familiar, unclothed modesty of show people. The communal consciousness was transmitted undefiled. Suckers for peeps were thwarted by posted signs of PRIVATE—KEEP OUT. The used-to-be dancers paid the rental fee, wrung out their towels, spat over each other's good shoulder for luck, and departed for the lonely clamor.

△

One long-ago day, Jimson surprised Ideal as she came out of a dressing room. Bearing a gift of a little orange flower, he waited, watching for her appearance. She was so confounded that she had no idea what to do with the flower. Should she wear it, carry it, or casually let it drop . . . ? How would the flower be explained to Adam who would assume that she had picked it or bought it on the way home? The gesture was guilty. The nighttime prayer's response was reaching out, shaking her outstretched hand. Jimson spoke giving images that pleased a dancing girl discovering the phenomenon of gesture.

Ideal thanked God for Jimson who responded know-ingly to her inspired, penetrating recapitulations on learning to dance. Nothing had been more frustrating than attempting to convey her experiences to one who sat blandly listening, lifeless, staring into space, accommodating. When all is said and done, this type of listener invariably says the wrong thing, something totally removed. Talking to the walls would be less exasperating.

Cuckolding Adam was not the thing to do any more . . . Ideal had wept and prayed for extrication. Bucketfuls. This phase was done. She was sick of imposition, excuses, fictitious people, and provoking arguments in order to storm out of the house—offended. She had drained the long bus ride, the trumped-up headache, the must get some fresh air, the urge to see a movie, the get some distance routines.

She had played the game and walked through the hometown girl's noctambulistic New York City dream of the penthouse overlooking the lagoon, the jazz musician, the foreign accent, the big-time hustler, the convertible car, the anonymity of a gay bar, the pensive novice, the paroled murderer, the movie star, the hired killer who wore an apron when he killed because he did not care for the trace of blood while he supped, the sentimental Jew boy for whom she almost left home. Ideal had practiced guile to the extent of swallowing aromatic flavors, and walking fast against the wind, unfurling the scent. She could fling open the door, take her stance, and carry it through without one accusation, or one demand for where she had been, what she had done. Comparison usurped admiration. Cuckolding siphoned sensuousness. Nothing was achieved out there . . .

△

Ideal took a good look at her lying mouth. How dare she let the mess fall from her lips. She was ashamed for having reduced Adam, amazed that he could not see beyond the transparency. Contemptuous of the nameless lovers for overriding or failing Adam, she never admitted to them that she, Ideal, had a husband lacking in cocksmanship. Why was it better to lie? Who was holding such a puritanical scepter, and better selected what was permissible? Ideal had become the child instinctively inventing reasons to retard the belt.

She hated herself for voluntarily hiding in the closet playing blind, vilifying the privilege of the detached being, the independent spirit. Lovers did not come forward to aspirate the dirt. Misrepresentation was their share, too. By further concocting a free soul who must get back home for responsible reasons, ingloriousness multiplied. Ideal was determined to resolve the chaos. She had to before the last degree of lowered-eyelid respect escaped. The polyerotic was flailing the sense out of the devil-will-get-you hometown girl. The people back home had told her so . . . Impatient dogs sniff the hind legs of bitches. Don't let him jiggle his paws against you. Tell him to get down. Go lie in his frantic corner. Bristle, pant his breath away. Wait until dog days to have his summer blood blanched.

Last night, the intention was not to be maudlin when Ideal asked Jimson if he remembered their coming together. Unaware of the stacked-deck capture, she accepted the orange flower and welcomed Jimson in the expiating guise of platonic attunement. Out of their expostulation of the Saturday night ball they created a self-styled sublimation, flatly refusing to embrace or to violate contaminated wedding vows. Virginity could renew itself. Tradition would be honored with forsworn statements of intention, if Jimson and Ideal could believe that touch would fasten them to time lasting longer than a night. "To get—is to blow," Jimson warned.

Luis had no notion of the zigzag depth of Ideal's involvement. They exchanged careful exhumations of the human life. They spoke softly, ate quietly, projected pure kindness from nine to five.

The light flashed on the telephone. Ideal turned aside, spoke low, reached for her purse, gave Luis the excuse. "I'll be back shortly," she said.

five

△

The mojo had backfired. Jimson was not waiting. Ideal tore off another layer of flesh, mumbling, "Got to get to the bottom of this." His telephone voice had sounded pleasant and clear of last night's tirade. Miscalculation averted Jimson's nature. To let him tell it, he was the exact, calm arrow that knew where it wanted to go, how to go about getting there without going at all. Looking up and down the street and name calling were wastes of time that striated the optic nerve and tired the neck. Time, they said, was the great healer. By what means would the cure occur? Jimson preached that the recuperation would be the result of Hippocratic mercy. Assuming the role of faith healer, time would excise our ill-founded pathology, leaving us ethereal creatures transfused with a changed fate, and awesome respect for our incisions. Ideal did not understand at all the act of mercy. She mistranslated it into pastoral parables, urban despotism, war-relief programs.

Loud, outspoken thoughts between two fellows standing near Ideal invaded her exercise. For a moment, she believed that the two were not an actuality, but a physical dichotomy of her own jag.

"Now, man, let me tell you one thing; money is it. Don't tell me about National Brotherhood Week and merciful love, having some appreciation for the good old United States and its rags to riches history. That lily-white jazz is for the birds, Yardbird (bless his soul), T Bird, flying away from here like a bird."

"Yes, but hear this, my man. All that you have just said goes back to the bread, the money. You have got to have it to qualify, to make your move. Understand? Well, all right."

Through street-corner conversation coincidental to the world, the two fellows were revealing between themselves who they were, what was on their minds.

"You've got to get ready, my friend. How do you think

you will qualify with no money, no ingenuity? Granted, you are not up the creek by yourself; because some ofays are unready for their own world. Some Negroes are unready for the white man's world—and that is where we live, brother. Some whites would die from natural causes if they were shuffled into our world. How many of us are ready for the world as it is created? How many of us are ready to peep another dimension and see things as they really are? Are you ready to drop your guard, my man? Are they ready to turn off the hose and come face to face with the facts of life? This is now, I tell you. Please see the light. Take a look, brother, it is shining on the facts.

"We have been birthed in the dark, suckled on degradation. We are the people of excessive sensitivity. Fact incenses us as we see it as it is. We are outside, detached, viewing the arena as eternal spectators evaluating the conquerors, uncovering their weaknesses. When we put them down, man, they are naturally put down. We have been taught to fear and idolize them, while despising ourselves. We have not been free to voice even our temperaments. We have been taking it out among ourselves, practicing among each other all that we resent, all that we have received. We have associated authority, liberation, right with white. The happy thought is that victims transcend masters. It is the time for us to perceive the power of violence, the might-and-right use of it. We have got to love ourselves and transform our butt kickings and lynchings into an irresistible energy. Our hotheadedness can charge us with a riotous, demonstrative impatience that will bring about our fateful change. We have got to denounce ignorant passivity; it has been worked out of us. We have one thing left—our souls, our true natures . . . the only undefiled, beautiful thing within us. That would be gone, too, if they knew how to rob us of it."

The two fellows were talking themselves onto the road. The fork in the path was vanishing, carrying with it the wish to have another obey. The corner doctrine's utility was traveling beyond that of being a wishful alternative. The generations of Negroes who had hid in the closet playing blind would have their visions restored. Those who had originated the image of the perennially smiling slave would have their joke clarified. Those who had shuffled along scratching and drawling, "I don't know, Boss," would have the question answered with language suited to the inquisitor.

"Wait a minute, brother, you are talking off the wall. You are getting too far out for me. Am I correct in interpreting your idea of salvation for us as a self-protective movement? Man, I have been colored all my life; and I cannot see that if we were the ruling majority we would forsake proselytizing by bloodshed, either. You lead me to believe that we would end the perpetuation of racism, abdicate violence and servitude. Who would perpetuate the voice of soulful rhythm and humming prayers? Taboo would be obliviated from our skins, relegating the myth of our exotic virility to a classless downtrodden. Does your movement make the people concede that . . . ? When we consider the odds against us, the fact of population the least considered, the nonviolent method is the only intelligent possibility."

98

"You amaze me, brother . . . You still love, fear, and honor King James's blue-eyed pink-faced Jesus of storefront churches, a God outside of the universe. Is it not time the classic table is turned? Who is caring for whom and why? We are still following the blue-eyed concept of the way. We have found compassion, wisdom, and restoring grace through his religion; but at last, thank God, the blacks are evolving through demonstrations of the word. We are turning our vindictive warriors' hearts toward the foe. We have been practicing narcissistically over the River Jordan; memorizing, embedding our retorts for years, for centuries, using each other as audience. What is at the bottom of our black hearts is coming out now, brother, be it calm or turbulent . . . it's here. So what if our fighting-hearted generation is killed in the streets? We must practice retaliation, so that our generation's generation will be free to practice your superhuman nonviolence of the abstract mind. In qualitative, enduring ways I would be less now if I had been born as my white brothers—liberated and equal . . . superb; but, paradoxically, they are envying us these soulful, suffering experiences. They are in search of contrition, challenge, protest. The whole world is on the walk. They have a valid protest; and, like ours, it is buried under ideologies festering with common good. All that is touching, but it is come too late. I am temporally welded to all that my black brothers and sisters have shown me to spit upon . . . in the name of salaam. How dare they suck our essence now in the name of brotherhood? Forging a free new world and singing hymns, Bible reading was their last disguise. How can

99

we be asked to accept or abide by this new face? Say, can you show me one qualitative achievement . . . ? Damn, we gave the world the only culture from America —jazz. Everything that they are which is renowned or enduring was taught to them by us and the Indians. They don't know anything but war and trying to mind the world's business."

"What is it that you are trying to tell me—nonviolence is more than a weapon or an effete weapon? I think you are wrong, my friend. We cannot get anywhere by fighting it out—pistols versus atomic bombs, outnumbered self-protective movements against Jim Crow courts, dogs and police forces. We will never make it. We have to adopt a revolutionary dogma and use it, not as a weapon to wound or to offend, but as a way, a guiding principle. We must extricate inhumanity in an establishment of society under the land's law. Faith in the Universal Law transfigures the chaos, enables us to envision liberation rather than annihilation. We must call world-wide attention to the derangement of the bigot. The nonviolent movement's leaders have imparted a courageous volition among us, which has never been exhibited before. Never have Negroes been as organized and so attuned to their kinship. Our division is subtracted . . . I have to give credit to your ideas and movement, though, brother. Through your teachings, there is a generated race pride and dignity, a catalyst that one must recognize. You have breathed life into sleeping men and groups of yawning conservatives who heretofore have been scared to breathe lest they wake up Mr. Whatishisname. The brothers have converted a vast number of black Americans who are not necessarily convinced of the tenets of the Protestant concept, but who are nonetheless relatives of the race, reckoning daily with the gray evil. Granted, there are those moments in which a man could allow the will of his brute force to smash asunder the aggravating face of superior idiocy. He would choke to death Jim Crow, then turn around and shoot it for stinking. But, oh my friend, we must be wise men who understand the Law, who understand that mind is all, that ignorance is the outlaw. We must see injustice related to the whole of mankind. The underdog is a universal animal without a definite phylum. We must die trying to realize the first cause, envisioning the effects of the discipline. The Law will be reconstituted as we transcend that intelligence which induces us to create weapons apart from ourselves. Of course our days are numbered, but, obviously, more than life we revere the Prince of Peace, the God of Love, the Karmi Yogi, Mahatma, Moses, Allah, Kali Shakti, Zoroaster, Sakyamuni, Yin Yang, Jesus. Name it anything as long as it points the way to peace, salvation, my brother. What is more gloriously immutable than Spirit? The tool must be equal to the task. Are we seeking, brother, the destruction of man or the destruction of the concept?"

Gospel lit up the corner. One of the fellows turned to a white man attentively listening to their conversation. He asked the white man if he felt free. The white man pondered the question for a minute and answered with a slowly declared, "Yes." He had never given the question much consideration. Of course he felt free; he had been born without the nightmare of proof.

"Yes, but tell me, white man, do you feel free beyond the effects of color and sex? What about that part of you which is formless and colorless, that part which is not concerned with sex, color?"

The black man's questions kept coming. "Is freedom an individual concern, responsibility? Could the knowledge spread? Would saying it aloud liberate us one and all? The people's ears that the good news did not reach —what of their enlightenment? If they are in the dark, does their ignorance prohibit our free attainment? As long as one is enslaved, are we all? What will we become when the last is freed? What must transpire? Why do we find it fulfilling to be keeper?"

The white man caught the yellow traffic light changing to green, and left in a hurry. The street-corner antagonists burst out laughing at their cruel accomplishment.

△

Jimson still had not come; he would have wondered what was going on, why Ideal seemed to be laughing with the fellows rather than at them. She had no business going down to their level, finding lunch-hour stockboys worthy of her attention. She was wrong to dignify them. She should have sneered at their ignorance and interrogation of the white man. The ignorance of such black boys was dangerous. They were not equipped to inundate the white man, thrash him, and make him like the thrashing. It was the degree of consciousness employed which was the factor that would bring about

102

the needed change. What did street-corner philosophizing serve? The essence was not standing on the corner overhearing the ultimatum. The essence was sitting behind a desk giving orders, planning cities, advertising youth, hygiene, and hope, appointing committees to investigate committees, closing the market, nominating candidates, revising textbooks, fixing prices, bargaining for wages, amending rules, slanting the news, developing trade, shipping out citizens to win wars, choosing daggers for best friends' backs.

She should have gone directly to the heart, the core, or silently awaited her man. Those two monkeys proved nothing but the garbage of unreadiness. Jimson would have employed the dialectic, clobbered the man with graybeard tactics. The man worked across the street as a carry-out clerk, wrapping sandwiches and sealing containers with vexing plastic tops.

Jimson would not have gotten out his greeting for being piqued by Ideal's communal laughter. He had told her time and time again not to lend herself to the banality of babblers. He had taught her well how to evaluate obvious worth. If she must speak out, she must consciously disguise her expression with the skull and crossbones, speak in plain English, reassuring the listeners that their outspoken sentiments were as distasteful as poison. The means by which Jimson was able to define character instantly were beyond the intuitive realm of the provincial Ideal. Was it through the cock of the hat, the stance, the vocabulary, the diction? The goddamitcocksuckershitmotherfuckinghells the two fellows expelled—exiled the tumult, coughed up the excessive sensitivity, choking them to death. Jimson, the clair-voyant, saw beyond superimposed manifestations of costume. They could have worn Sweet Orrs or Stetson shoes; Jimson would not have let go his analysis. The costume could have been fashioned of Russian sable, unborn mink. The conversation could have been conducted from a podium or a Rolls-Royce; informing the listening of the colored lady who poured pink tea for guests displaying genteel manners while attending an RSVP soiree "in" such and such an avenue; and what he said, she said, and they wore. Jimson disallowed them the endowment of quality or change. That they attempted to bank weekly, discern differences, request quality, afford indulgences, would have impressed or softened Jimson's appraisal not one iota. They still remained the white man's emulation, his household joke. Their newly attained elegance confused artificiality with naturalism, flamboyance with flair, transference with imitation. Whether it was participation in work, play, brotherhood, or worship, Jimson derided the people for their overdressed attendance. Throughout the hypothetical categorization of the banal babblers, Ideal tried to formulate the theorem by which she could state and prove Jimson's monomania.

The banal babblers would have gladly relieved her of her problem. They, too, would have evaluated their initial look at Jimson. He would have been the Greenwich Village bearded neurotic who sucked up under ofays, too slick to work, did not have a dime, and lived in unreality escaped from his roots. They would have bet each other that he was the know-it-all unregistered voter laying up with a white girl who acted as his emissary into the local avant-garde. This same white girl was poorer and dumber than he was, homely; and impatiently awaiting the moment to rub color in his face while bleeding him of his virility, transforming him into a subjective, one-dimensioned phallus too lame to stand and call her by name. Her name was secondary to her color. "Man, I have got myself a white girl . . ." At the end of day, the banal babblers would have surmised that the bearded stranger bolted his door and, in unison, he and his white girl insulated each other with hushed avowals of sameness, untold soul, common contempt for his people, a liberal view of moderation, the amount of love and money needed to defend isolation.

The three, saying not a word, would have taken a second, doubting look—rechecking the validity of their instinctive evaluations. They would have been reassured, satisfied. No one warranted the haloed appraisal. All three were fugitives from the Bottom, vowing to hurry their metamorphosis. Identity with subjection was a coincidence that must be shed. To don the store-bought suit was an eye-opening avowal of the metamorphosis. The change of clothes from overalls to a long-trousers suit, from bandana to modish hat, from sackcloth to mohair, was one layer closer to the amalgamating adornment, to becoming someone rather than a thing called boy. Deprivation created compensation.

△

Luis Pagan must have just left the office. Ideal sniffed his citrus smell. A note on her desk told her Jimson had phoned, would meet her at home. It was just as well that she and Jimson missed each other. His sober tone inter-mixed with the freedom-now! boys would have been the dissonant crash of the last word. At this moment, the whole lot could go to hell. The file folder was yet un-opened. She had spent the day engaging in every ac-tivity except the one for which she was being paid. Not a blessed soul, Luis, Jimson, or the orators, was lifting the burden from her back. When the landlord for-warded eviction notices, it was the dear old boss who signed the requests for advances on her paycheck. Jim-son supplied the cynical good humor that blockaded the apartment with a boyish leave-me-alone. Objections were flimsy, non-negotiable means with which to ad-monish bill collectors and kindhearted immigrant grocers. Protest and pace were falling from everybody's lips, pouring down the ear, only to be secured within a bank vault the moment there was a seeming answer to their private prayers.

The world was fighting for its life. Dilapidated, con-demned house had been deafened by the beseeching moans of indigents and immigrants hovering in the same corners, cursing the same conditions during times be-fore the present dwellers. Neither of the street dis-senters had initiated an action for distending wrinkled bellies, clothing the shivering, housing the homeless. The newfangled taste of freedom was driving people crazy. They had forgotten their place, and jumped up and down demanding to be counted. The few people stood unaroused; awaiting the pause, soliciting the strong-in-heart who were not seduced from the veritable intention. Slanderous accusations, black-mouthed, white-toothed lies, dispossessed leaders, foaming phonies, and the newly arrived stampeded the few people, claiming, "No one has ever done a damned thing for me! You grab all you can and slam your door . . ."

Ideal could settle down and get her duties done, or resignedly decapitate herself with a floor-size double-duty fan. The resolution marked time by an inaudible voice faltering somewhere inside an impenetrable cell.

Duty parades in and out of mind every day that the Good Lord sends. It finds people ready-made for the order it wishes to give. Some duties a dog would not be ordered to perform. His lack of dexterity and comprehension negate his capacity to execute those tasks for which people have been made. He lies in the undisturbed corner, hovering over his feces, growling indignantly at those who carry out the unspeakable duty. Human kindness is his reward for a tongue-lapping, tail-wagging loyalty. Dumbly, he stands and receives accolades of two pairs of rubber booties, rubber bones, periodic inoculations, pedicures and clippings, government-inspected nourishment, tartan plaid doggie coats, golden-studded leashes, lozenges to correct his breath, blue ribbons, and a prepaid, certified burial plot assuring his master that he will go to his rest in a segregated hunting ground. The duty-bound people console the living and sweep up the dust of master's one true friend. It serves them right for broadcasting the dogma, " 'Tis true we do a lot of things we do not like to do, but someone has to do it. It must be done and, at least, it is honest . . ." The incantation is hummed and designed to coincide with the everlasting sunrise. Arising, the people repeat the dogma, immunizing themselves for duty's call. The unclean spirit lies in bed while the sun shines, entrancing ogres to keep the people in a purging lather. Novices are led by the hand—away from the domain of satanic uncleanliness. Boys are ushered to the backyards, cellars, and broom closets; girls to the kitchens, sink, chamber, laundry. Tasks are available to suit the prowess. Play, wonder, and the childish inclination toward impulse are pruned. Time enough for nonsense.

The pruning ritual antedates the age of reason so that when the children are led into the compulsory classroom, the manual training, family-care curricula hardly receive undivided attention. Those who have stubbornly managed to wonder why, or to be transported by IF during their tasks, are promoted into apple-green classrooms with walls bearing decadent pendulum clocks, approved portraits of the powdered-wig father.

Exuding a contempt for humanity which supplants an equal disdain for knowledge, celibate teachers ignore the excellence of oral transmission; directing, instead, the young minds to thumb through and absorb endless yellowed pages of illiberal history, mathematical story problems, geographical information presented through remote summer excursions to a white-haired old lady's summer home, where spotted dogs romp with wholesome children, and barnyard animals perform abundantly their punctual function. A ready-made farmhand mesmerizes the wholesome children with tales of friendly Indians.

Duty in no way honors the book learning; preferring, instead, to bestow honor upon those who primarily proclaim its right-mindedness. Chastisement for those choosing to slight duty is volunteered by a daytime-sleeping devil. Rebuking ranges from common curse, dessert denial, sleep without supper, domestic imprisonment, face slapping, head whipping. The instruments employed are designed for the foot, the pressing iron, the tree, the laundry, the haberdasher, the baseball diamond, the rosebush, the klannish torturer, the lion tamer. Methods are devised to detain self-protecting, head-shielding criminals from cheating jealous duty of its eye for an eye.

Sacrifice, guilt, initiative, responsibility join in the declamation, and slash across the back to the rhythmical beat of "You are going to obey me or else." The handwriting exercises being taught to the young minds come into play. They are instructed to make every minute count by writing notes to an absentee executioner characterizing their transgressions against duty; requesting in formal language that they, the accused, be beaten half to death before daybreak. The young minds pray for morning . . . and winds that will blow the posted notes into an overlooked corner. In order that the victims keep still, receive the hurt, swear never to do it again, they are horsewhipped publicly in front of school friend's gaping eyes, during the pause of day in which the whole neighborhood is quiet and able to hear; stripped of store-bought, hard-earned clothing, and face down—prone upon two chairs with their heads pushed through one end, while their feet dance through the other. "Yes! I, or better still we, will beat the living life out of you in the name of obedience, respect for authority and our common dream for you."

109

Duty, overcome by the trenchant act of punishment, is unable to hear the lie created out of spontaneous preservation, or the truth gasping between breaths of "Please, I won't do it any more."

Admonishing the victim to stop its whining, clean up its bloody mess, unimpeachable duty retreats, undismayed, exhausted with fellow feeling. Throughout the discipline, duty remained on a self-forgiving plane. There was no need to question or justify its action; if anything, the punishment was not thorough enough. The victims should have been molested, hanged from trees; their innocent prayers bombed into fragments. The flagellated body gathered its members from the puddle streaming across the floor, whimpering incessantly, since it had been lastly attacked for feigning histrionics. The bruises festered. The iridescent welts glared, maiming the victim's capability of lying down to salt, to loathe, or to relish its condition. It was over and forgotten—thought the executioners. The victim was guilty of capricious inefficiency, willful defiance, infantile irresponsibility. After all, they had not worked like dogs all day, taken abuse from incompetent henchmen who dared them to talk back, come back home to unrewarding, overdue shelters, to be annoyed by unstrung puppets vexing them with woodenheaded anarchy and wilted flowers not sprouting the flowers of no conflict.

When pharisaical righteousness expounds its mealy-mouthed, duty-bound dissertations, martyrs know they died for nothing; victims achieve the absolute orgasm.

six

△

Halt! Cool it. Jimson spelled out the meaning of his
telephone call. Bless his heart, Lord, he had found a job.
He was going to work; but the decision did not cause
Ideal to jump up and dance, grab him around his neck,
doing a jig to whatever IT is; since the announcement,

naturally, was accompanied by an infernal red tape sealing the condition with, "Stay home, Ideal, and just be my wife." Any man deserving the name wanted his wife to do just that—stay at home and be his mistressmother.

Jimson was sick of Ideal's chronic dispraise. Ideal would not have to do a damned thing for him another further time. He was the man whom she would respect. He would show her. Her never-ending tirade broadcast opinionated statistics, documented evidence of the black man's inefficiency, his unwillingness to work, to stand up and be counted. It fluctuated between hearsay, resentment, and American success.

What was her contention this evening? Why no cheers and buying spree? That Jimson get off his haunches and amount to something was what she had been insisting upon. Staying at home signified an unengaging existence. "Fear is negative desire," Jimson said—"that which we do not want." Ideal did not want mirror gazing, window watching, coffee drinking, cigarette smoking, the unendurable domestic whirligig, eating only to wash dishes, washing dishes only to eat, making, unmaking the bed, straightening up, sweeping out, laundering, sudsing up, motions that did not bring Jimson back in a flash, polish prudence, nor cleanse hope. Mars rotated alongside Venus flailing the impulse out of glamour girls. Ideal was afraid of Jimson. She had learned better than to sit at the impermanent feet of Jimson. He swore, "When he was born, he had big eyes and big feet; so he walked all over the world and saw everything."

Every stitch she owned, she had worked somewhere long and hard to have it. Santa Claus had cooled his jolly visitation. Ho Ho Ho. New York winters whipped her spring raincoat to waterproof shreds. She had a lovely bunch of buttons, though. Flair surrendered its seasonal punch while the Hawk held forth for umpteen days. The last real winter coat her father had sent to her—sight unseen, but envisioned during a chattering call home.

If Jimson went to work, she would criticize, see the nest for what it barely was. If he stayed at home, she bitched, blessed him out. Jimson had several favorite lectures. One began, "I will teach you to take care of yourself"—the liberal's world-wide doctrine of local assistance. You are not prepared to manage yourself. You need our help; so that we are assured that you will govern your affairs in the right white way, my way. To make us beam with benevolence, you must repeat after us, "We were lost souls seeking a lost god, although now we have knowledge of the way. By following your system, we are free from poverty, ignorance, disease. Health, success, infinite happiness are our daily rewards. Choice, we leave to you who know our needs far better than we . . ."

Secure in the revolution, the liberals moved onward proselytizing other regions, waiting patiently, assisting locally those direly in need of Help! The areas to be developed were determined by the total count of audible drumbeats, chants to unknown deities, downhill lines upon graphic charts indicating social disease, unemployment, illiterate illegitimacy.

113

Red-feathered angels of mercy descended in the wake of klieg lights. God bless them. They had come to locally assist. They manned comfort stations, birth control clinics, training camps, social agencies, mass meetings, round-table discussions. Freely, they passed out redemption and illustrated self-help pamphlets depicting progress. Tabulated reports revealed dense accumulations of blight. No need to worry . . . Help would stand guard to alleviate conditions, to shuttle the needy through barbed-wire fences toward the zone of the better welfare. The essential cure lay breeding goldbricks for the democratic capital, fattening paper words in commissioned reports, researching projects for liberal volunteers. Vox Pop(u-li). The ticker tape protected itself against the noisy boom of crash when peace talked in a voice like the sound of money.

The lecture did Ideal no good. She had heard it time and time again. Gabriel had blown the sluggard out of bed. Jimson had to be kidding. He was not, though. He had found the suitable job, one in which his talents could be exposed and disciplined—all during the man hours. Five days a week he would relinquish to an esoteric library, cataloguing, stocking, shipping books. The mecca, the intellectual salon, was furnished with ordered shelves of the timeless wisdom, subtle incense, bronze mirrors, Agni's flame, Byzantine icons, kinky-haired Buddha, prayer beads, and yarrow stalks. Temple bells rang in-out the honorable guests.

Footsteps walked in the seven directions. A prayer rug absorbed Jimson. Lichi, sake, zori, tea. The thousand and one things catapulted the poet, beckoned him sit in

114

the bamboo garden, contemplate ascensions of underground shoots. Jimson let go the carcass, became vegetarian.

The library was entrusted to a bird-faced austere old spinster. The late founder could not have appointed a more devoted servant. With Virgoan exactitude, Rheba undertook her duties, leaving no picayune detail to nettle her staff. Rheba might have been one of the old world's more elegant dowagers; instead, she was the nostalgic pressed flower, the wiry blue-veined overseer, the cow-posturing camp, resigned from the gay life. Coquetry's last vestige was wearing hair . . . Rheba combed it into a rigid chignon, never pinning her hair into a balanced ball, but just ever so slightly off center. Having been overawed by a rampant matriarch-propagating middle-class abstention, Rheba embodied the middy-bloused tradition of the private church school. The culture befitted her mother's narrowed aspiration. Rheba was qualified to overturn ancient stones, recollecting the historical trespassers without varying a bloody fact; guide pilgrims across country, while pointing out still-standing dwellings, the renowned residents they had housed; rattle off even the minor poets, detect symphonies by the opening bar. Her memory was a musty airless museum, an embroidered attic of colonial warriors, saints and phantoms, velum parchment, belles-lettres, artifact, an engraved menu of regional tastes. Worn out by obsolescence and benefactors refusing to pass on, Rheba booked passage on the utopian *Mayflower*, first class.

The work was not hard. The boss was not mean.

115

Rheba granted Jimson the seclusion to do his work leisurely. He took the liberty of visitor appraisals, browsing, and whistling his lonesome tune . . . something about a colored man having troubles down in old Hong Kong. A suffocating cubicle functioned, at once, as staff kitchen and Jimson's bureau. Bubbling pots lent further aroma to the sweatbox. Jimson tore off sheets of brown paper, wrapped books, cut cord, licked stamps, stacked his booty on a little dolly cart, then took off daily for the post office walk. Status never colored Jimson's face nor batted his eyes. He acknowledged the job's necessity. Knowing what he wanted to gain from the labor, he willingly performed the manual tasks. His hands freed his brain to think. The acquisition was unhampered. But throughout the man hours, Jimson overheard the but, the big BUT. The word conjoined actions, varied appearances, altered decisions, wracked poor Jimson with dualistic thoughts.

Speculation had paralyzed Jimson, until he was unable to withstand another theory. He wanted to be done beating around the bush and, simply, to cleave the middle to be done with floundering. If he had to read each text in the library, absorb every printed word, discard perennial and novel tenets, he would disentangle himself from superfluity. He would float up the Hudson sitting on a lotus blossom, if all else failed, if a push turned into a shove. Jimson wanted to know and had sense enough to know that he did not know. From a child, "I don't know" is a valid, acceptable answer. An adult answering with this same statement is snubbed, regarded as a nincompoop, a fool, a naïve fat-headed simpleton. Conceit and stupidity come to the rescue answering with incredible triteness, exasperating lies, polysyllable vocabularies, and fishy-eyed looks straining to avoid looking the questioner in the eye. Numbers and percentages are quoted.

Quantity is employed, since quantity has grown to outweigh quality. What we do not know is analyzed. Ambitious men lie awake scheming while we sleep, deciding how our ignorant innocence will best be exploited. In the morning, we are disinherited, buried in pleated satin-lined boxes symmetrically designed to contain our gross, decaying dimensions.

Rheba studied Jimson. Jimson studied Rheba. Neither of them scrutinized each other in that way which untried lovers taste the words pouring out of each other's mouths, those unutterable sounds locked behind up-and-down glances. Neither of them fleshed against each other in the face of destiny staggering their forms, nor supported each other with proffered arms while walking that clumsy walk which stumbles all over itself, its timid, gawky self; nor were they seduced into walking backwards out the door, or sensitive to that breath which falters short of a kiss. Falling in love is something else . . .

By the sound of the clacking abacus balls, the typewriter's marginal peal, the rumbling desk drawer, the slapping soles on the parquet floor, the periodic apple munching, Jimson could detect each of Rheba's functions—just where she would perch or flit next. Sometimes from his cubicle, he could hear her stop just the other side of the wall—her breathing controlled, hesitant,

117

as though she were holding it to more easily snoop. His poignant tune would become more resonant; the whistled blues blew straight at the estimated spot where, surely, her ear must be glued. That would get her, send her swooping back to her withered limb.

Rheba could not comprehend Jimson's sly advantage. Guerrilla stratagem. He was nursed on the finesse, the camouflaged hunter, the niggah in the woodpile . . . She knew he had to be in his cubicle. He had better be. She was paying him to be there. It was useless to track his movements; his shoes were sponge-bottomed, his occupation sedentary. Jimson coveted and cultivated the role of the enigma, the bearded genie, the omniscient spectator. Rheba would have to play the game according to the book, if she wanted to peep at Jimson's hole card. She did not have the heart to approach him head-on, ask him directly whatever it was she thought she needed to know. Like a taxidermist, hope had stuffed Rheba into a pitiful lackluster birdface who assumed the frozen desires lurking in her lifeless stare could be instantly revived by any seer attuned to odious sentiment. Rheba had no sympathetic prophet in Jimson. Revival meetings he had left behind. He could taunt her to death, salt her unasked inquiries until she dissolved into the egg. Heartless, cold was he whom Rheba had decided to take under her wing. If she had fancied a Nubian slave, a strapping black buck to fan away flies, to massage varicose veins, to induce sweet breezes, to answer, "Yes, my lady, how right you are" . . . well, Rheba had made the unforgettable wrong choice of her waning life.

As soon as Jimson finished his search among the books, took one and went off to read, birdface came hopping behind, taking note of what he had chosen, what it was he wanted to know. She knew the stock from A to Z, having scanned them all in order to better sell them or review them for monthly circulars. Here was the way Jimson could be had. Now she could properly ask him to define his dream, the source of his volition . . . unearth his dark presence.

Rheba had had enough of this taciturn recluse. Jimson must lower his burden, lighten his load. An intelligent exchange of frustrations would be better for them both. Everyone knows that talking it out of the soul helps. Florence Nightingale turned over. Calling upon her last dreg of wile, Rheba began her obvious salvation by adding extended greetings: "How are you, Jimson? By the way, that book you are reading happens to be one of my favorites—almost my bible."

The greetings developed into brushing by him among the shelves, just happening to recall another tidbit, taking her tea in the cubicle, inviting him to be introduced to the honorable guests. The woman was driving the man to distraction with unsolicited attention. If she wanted to do something, really give him something, she could simply offer him something actual, please, like money, a decent wage commensurate to his education, equal status accompanied by equal pay, privacy. Jimson was an old soul roaming the earth since the beginning. To him, the waiting game was recreation. In his next time around, he had been promised that he would reach the stage of tenderness and shed retribu-

119

tion, withdraw vengeance. In his roaming, he met a Jew who told him that fatigue brings tenderness . . .

That Rheba thought that Jimson could define his dream, supply the questions to her pat answers, amused, tickled, and flattered him—for a moment. Why should she see him as sphinx? Rheba and all whom she represented had attempted to annihilate every soul brother on the face of the earth. They had stood for centuries on top, above the soul brothers—never, though, at eye level. They could not. They would have gazed back at their numbed skulls, their heinous greed, their mania.

The scrawny-legged witch ought to have marked time, locked herself in her ozone box, contemplated her dilettante navel. She was unready to endure the apocalypse for which she begged Jimson. He had suffered his own, the natural, and the imposed. Maybe it was love and affection the great white mother desired, love bites from a shackled leg. Maybe she had eavesdropped upon the great white father's retired-to-the-den discussions which, invariably, centered around the incredible circumference and length of the brother's member, the number of times he could will its ascension, the well-known fact that women could never leave him. For what other reasons could black men wear a mustache? Jimson was not her god and he knew it. He was not thinking about forgiving her for a damned thing— actual or imagined. God and mother possessed unconditional love. He was a man and trying his best to act like one, if the old hag would just leave him alone. Jesus Christ! he could see why you passed on by a hankering, swooning, thigh-spreading bunch of frustrated dimwits.

If Rheba wanted forgiveness, eradication of guilt, restoration of self-respect, it was best that she find herself an identical confessor. Jimson could not hear her. Long live disparity!

Rheba was reduced to tears, torn to pieces. She had done all that she could be expected to do. She hired Jimson, paid him on time, asked him to do nothing beneath him, introduced him to her guests, praised his intelligence to the hilt. But Jimson had cheated, violated the unmentioned agreement, bitten the hand that fed him. Rheba had gone out of her way to make him feel at home, treating him as she did not treat her own kind. Inwardly, she berated Jimson for foul play, for not fawning over her kindness, seeing in-the-moment her difference.

He was being too hasty in asking for total assimilation, parading his private sickness, suggesting that she respond as he, and take up arms, cry the woe. Rheba wondered if she would like Jimson, be as fascinated by him, or willing to receive his indignations and effronteries had he been not a Negro, but just another white boy. He would not have been the same. Why and how is color contributed to his magnetism was a notion refusing to become her problem. She shoved it out of mind. That she did what she did, said what she had said, was enough—more than necessary. Rheba had saved herself. All by himself, Jimson could have the devilish job of answering the question, changing her mind, making over the country to suit his dream.

In Jimson's secret heart he envied Rheba the license to stand up, blatantly question, and spontaneously think

121

she was first in line—to oppose, to express opinion, to criticize. Whether she be received as lofty, profound, absurd, pretentious, or stupid, she had the privilege. Up to this day, he had not taken the same freedom; except on emotional occasions, in sequestered quarters. Ineffectual listeners heard him out and gave him replies of "I don't know." Most of them had lost the irretrievable right to blurt out, saying precisely what they meant by exploiting, draining dry the one among the four—the freedom of speech.

A Negro has been instructed since stepping foot on the land to choose his words, watch his diction, precheck his grammatical construction. Say it just as the white (if it is to him that you would address your comments). Lightning will strike a black man for uttering some things. The white man will douse him with kerosene, set him on fire for telling it "like" it is. Be cool. Do not let them get the best of you. Their everlasting great defensive argument is that you are a child of the spirit, emotionally unready for their elliptical language and reason. You ought to be glad . . . The exotic eats us up, feeds upon us like a paunchy carnivore. Anyway, everybody knows that nothing black, red, brown, or yellow has sent anybody anywhere near the moon. We are still baby and fool enough to be fooling around down here on earth trying to figure out what happened; why it is that we are the last to catch up. Peace is white-faced. Aggression is yellow.

Someone told Jimson last night that he loved the world's colored leaders because they quoted poets, wrote poems, and were heartbroken with human nature as it is practiced here on the planet Earth. Somewhere beyond this point, on this printed page, the world's next leaders sit writhing in agony against the will to oblivion. They have not, yet, the solution. Neither has Jimson. What will be the position for the maimed to adopt? An unremovable cataract blackens their optimism, thwarts their retaliating with love. They see beyond the touching propaganda. They are the transforming populations—seven times a trillion, zillion. This same someone told Jimson he would register and vote for poets; if some white-housed candidates would only open up their souls and spout some. Jimson hoped red-necked, uniformed goons, double-jointed bastards would come quick and lock him up. Take him out of his sweat-box. Put him in Leavenworth, convict him for seeing things as they are, stifle him for feeling it as it is. Incongruity filled with air pockets, politically expedient, big-business endorsed, klanning and planning leaves here the same.

We either get ourselves together or we don't, stay in the world or give it up. Jimson wanted to reign supreme, manly; and get up off his knees, stop begging among the down-and-out.

Without back-stepping one tread, but steadily stepping all over Jimson's way, Rheba persisted in talking the incessant, insignificant talk of old women—that conversation which is punctuated by oral mannerisms, gum sucking, lip wetting, tongue flicking, food-particle removing. Further, the talk uncovered the unperforated, unballed split, the unscrewed crack, the unfilled belly.

"Love," she said, "one another" . . . For what?

Perennially, Jimson had observed the loving multitude. By watching its public and familiar manifestations, his loving eye had shrunk to the minute close-range perspective of a Lilliputian.

"Oh hell, I have had just about enough of this hag. I quit," Jimson said.

seven

△

"Right now, this is our point in the universe. From this place, Jimson, I extend greetings to you. Good day. Stop, please, right here at this articulated juncture. Let us draw a single breath from it, dear heart, while we are here. Distance is divided by such simple steps in time and space."

125

Willfully, Ideal traveled through distance in a sulphur colored to reconstruct an image that would bring to mind another's face, another's attitude. That any time was real to her hinged on the possibility of being able to discern time and distance. "I must court neither this, nor that. I shall become interested in actuality," Ideal said aloud to the looking-glass seer. Time and distance overwhelmed memory's fervor. Time and distance were probing the very fragile depth of Jimson and Ideal's intimacy. Across her mind's eye, each moving disappearing flash of Jimson counterfeited itself.

Could time and distance have seduced them out of their ecstasy, out of their exclusive, fey-living selves? To climb to that stage at which there is no more romance is such a miserable last straw. Somewhere along the way back home, in the same moment, Jimson was untangling strings of feelings. Telepathic nostalgia was making both of them so weary of themselves. Should they not have warm tears easing their vision's gaze into a recent short past? Should they not have ears listening in the darkness, awaiting the last word? Should their souls not come bursting stars, colors, shrieks, booms of fireworks down a long dark hall echoing and reverberating AUM against its walls?

Walk, Jimson, step, my friend, over here. Grass along the esplanade became his meditating seat. A passing soldier relieved his mind of his quite piquant questions. The soldier, bending down to Jimson, asked, "Are you looking for a hero warrior?" Slightly startled, Jimson answered him with a breath that did not speak his language. "He is over there across the park under the

ginkgo tree. You know, the one that belongs to Ideal."
Coincidence shook Jimson. His true feelings hid.

Hush! a parade was coming. Yes. Without seeing at
all, Ideal could tell who was doing the drumming and
walking along to beat the band. Colored hands were
beating out a pulse native to her own. The sound of
Jimson's walk was different this evening. It resounded
with the finality of never-will-go-marching-again. Concrete and asphalt in New York has a way of becoming
animate. It whiplashes from the Achilles tendon to the
medulla oblongata; jarring, drumming, and deforming
the pedestrian until he becomes capable of doing nothing other than searching upon the ground, prospecting
for El Dorado, stalking a dropped coin. With each put-
ting down of the heels, the whole body sinks farther
down into an abysmal muck. Walking has a triplet
count. On step one, our bodies are thrown into space.
Accompanied by a down gush of breath, for a second,
we are fallen. On steps two and three, recovering, we
upright ourselves onward toward whatever our destina-
tions are. Walking these same movements day in and
day out, over the same ground, going toward the same
objectives, wears out the best of soles. The cerebellum
demands that we stop, go harbor ourselves within whatever our nests might be, and renounce the state—if just
for an hour. The sound of a crabby dictating cerebellum
exuded from Jimson's coming-back-home walk this evening.

Jimson walked straight to the dresser without saying
so much as Hello. He took a tube of lipstick and scrawled
across the wall the words—I WANT. He would have to

127

choose the reddest, most indelible, kissproof lipstick Ideal owned. The funereal mauve clashed dissonantly with the yellow-orange sun.

"Jimson, Jimson, darling . . . what on earth are you doing? What is the meaning of that? You act as if you have lost your mind. Are you crazy? How am I going to wash that mess off?"

"Quite the contrary, my love. I have just found my mind again. I am sure that you have enough sense to see that I have had it, that I have quit my job. Purposely, I have written those two plain words on the wall. Look at it. What does it say? I want, you want, he wants, we want, they want. It is the root, Ideal, the cause. This suit of flesh is not my nature. To arouse my flesh at birth proves only the perfection of the physical. It does not want—I will. My father used to say, 'Have you ever had your wants to hurt you?' And don't you dare wash off one mark, one curlicue. Contemplate it, rather than your whip-handle.

"Shall I tell you my most subjective thoughts? Shall I tell you of the reflection that I see and criticize whenever I look in that mirror? You are able to surmise my daily state. Yes? Can you surmise that all my life I have been dissatisfied with conditions, especially those that I have created for myself? Can you tell that, always, I am saving my best for a period that I am only able to imagine? Can you tell, according to the psychologists who categorize American Negroes as paranoiac-schizophrenic, that I am in a great battle with what is and what is not? Jesus Christ was a poor man. Can you tell that the misinterpreted Judaeo-Christian ethic coupled with Americana renders us lustful regarding money? God has become faith in one's schemes to get rich quick. Can you tell that I judge by means of one's indwelling essence? Can you tell that I am charmed by grace, self-confidence, accomplishment, a hero, a heroine, by the animal revealing itself in love's privacy only? Can you tell that I would kill hypocrisy? Can you tell the condition and the medium of exchange which I would offer Satan were he to come calling upon me with his mythical proposition? Can you tell that I have paralyzed myself? Can you tell that I do not see the light or the forest? Can you tell me what makes me continue living a life that is not fulfilling? Can you tell why you need to castrate me? Why I need to be castrated? Can you tell why I am not engaged in daily actions that would affect my desires? Can you tell what about me is fact and what is fancy? Can you tell what I want? Can you tell if what I want is what I need? Can you tell me if need and desire are in unison? I am awaiting my truth, Ideal. Come on, now, I am counting on the change, the Apocalypse. What are the elements of the rock foundation?"

Ideal did not know whether to get up or sit down, lie down or stand up, speak up or shut up. Jimson had blown his top.

"Oh, Daddy, I believe. Oh, Daddy, I love. What can I say that will suffice, make everything all right? Nothing, Jimson, nothing. Just please say that it is not my fault. Rheba did it to you, the world, America, Papa Boo, time, anything but me. Come on now, Daddy, get in the bed, hold me, tell me what happened today,

129

tell me that you are not blaming me. I am not used to you this way. I thought that I was the evil, crazy one between us. Oh, dear God, please do not let him hurt this way. My man says his prayers, sucks my soul, beats my ass, tells me truth, talks love with his eyes, and is so good while being so mean."

All of a sudden, Jimson whirled around, grabbed Ideal out of bed and began beating, raining down upon her head with palms and fists mimicking the rhythmic outpouring of his can-you-tell. Between screams of "Jimson, stop it and please leave me alone," he bellowed that she respond, fight him like a man. If this was what Jimson needed in order to calm down, take away his throe, Ideal would respond. Flinging her whole body against him, flailing, she bit, clawed, kicked, and held on with her not-too-dear life to any part of his wailing body that extended itself. Why did she do as she was told, Lord? With a virgin energy, Jimson trounced upon her as if she were original sin, the cause of all suffering, the original slave trader, the civil service executioner, the stoker of the furnaces for nine million Jews. Calling upon the neighbors served no purpose, none whatsoever. They were used to tenement blues and love taps. Somehow the furniture joined in the fight. Plaster dropped shrapnel. Floorboards moaned. Glass shattered. Blood decorated the walls. A corner reached out and grabbed Ideal. Pushing the bed into the safe corner, mashing her legs until her body bent over flattening against the barricade, Jimson spit in contempt, panting the words, "You just don't love me, Ideal. That's all . . ."

△

130

Dark glasses serve two kinds well—vipers and black-eyed women. Jimson had not been home since that evening. For the sake of the continuation of their little romance, this misrepresentation of fact, the telephone rang out of her morning sleep. Although he had almost beat daylight into her, Ideal invoked fate and cried, "Call for me, call for me, call for me. I am your answer. You are the prayer. Black man, come on strong like. Spring, slappity slap. You are a roaring jaguar. Its wind belches exhausted air. Love defecates upon our bed's soul. Oh, Jimson, you sweet soft daddy turning into sweat, make wires ring this day."

Jimson was staying with friends. He wanted Ideal to come as quickly as possible. In less than a moment, Ideal was searching up and down a remote block on the Lower East Side. Jimson was locked up in one of those brick boxes. When she arrived at the door, Jimson invited her to enter. "The door is not locked," he said. On a corner of a bed, without a stitch of clothes, Jimson sat, groomed, greased, gleaming, and writing something down on a single sheet of paper. Sunlight streaked his greased flesh, accentuating every vein, muscle, fiber. Oil glistened in his hair. His aura, dancing in and out of a rainbow arc, splintered into stunning prisms. A tranquil breeze stirred the curtain, wafted through the room, atomizing the fruit-luscious scent, flowered the walls, smoked the scene with floating heat.

"Ideal, I am going to kill myself and I want you to witness it. Have a seat while I finish writing this last poem to you, please."

Well, Lord have mercy, he was not pretending. A

131

knife lay next to him shining with freshly stropped determination. As Jimson watched Ideal take notice of the blade, gasp, freeze in space, attempting to utter words of inquiry or prohibition, he repeated his command of sit down and wait.

Impulse choked the courage and escape out of her. Stupefied, Ideal stood crippled, awaiting the moment for Jimson to be done with his poem. Disarm, breath, prism, light, oil, beard, skin, brick box, help police, run away, don't look, why, theatrics, cold steel, corner of an unfamiliar bed, a tree-of-life bedspread, a nearly concluded poem, a lover with the blood dribbling out of him, a dumfounded, incoherent girl testifying to Saint Peter or Justice—bluffed and prompted Jimson to hurry with the poem, end it all, or laugh it off.

Jimson flung down the pen saying, "What is the use? Someday, Ideal, you will understand."

She never would be able to understand; nor would Jimson be able to rationalize the next minute. As he pressed the knife down into his wrist, Ideal leaped across the room, snatched the blade, and splattered blood. With blood spilling at every tenth count, she had become wounded in the great suicide attempt.

Deduction did not let her know until hours later that the blade's ineffectual, noncutting edge was turned away from his wrist. With a handful of five bleeding fingers, Ideal rushed out of the apartment. In heart-attacking panic, she turned in each direction, flurrying toward the nearest sign of help. A lackadaisical salesclerk pointed toward a phone booth. Frenzied pulsation dialed the police. Her brain stretched and snapped; her nerves, unwinding telepathically, ordered the police to make a faster move, get in their car, roll faster the wheels, arrive now, not as soon as possible, but now.

Who should come casually past the shop window? Of course, Jimson . . . In view of her hemorrhaging hand and sticky gushing blood, Ideal could envision no other sight of Jimson other than prostrate before his Maker. He had to be dead, damn! Please do not let him see me standing here. Make him go on by. The Lord takes care of fools and babies. The sirenless siren, the wheelless wheels, the motorless motor of the squad car could be intuited, if not heard, as the law turning into the block upheld the name of New York's finest . . .

What a ridiculous story to explain. While the officers rushed into the apartment, Ideal ran behind them trying to explain the trite story.

"He is not here, I tell you. I just saw him going down the street. Yes, he was alive. Yes, I called saying that a man was committing suicide. He didn't though. I stopped him. No, I was not trying to kill myself. My hand got hurt trying grabbing the knife away from him. I wanted to run away; I wanted to see him kill himself; I wanted you to stop him, to save his life; but I am the only one who shed blood. That's weird, isn't it, officer? I should have known it was too arranged, too poetic, to be true. No, I do not want emergency treatment. I want the hand to heal slowly before his eyes. I hope gangrene sets in, that it has to be amputated, that I die of blood poisoning."

"Look, lady, we cannot leave you standing here like this. You have to calm down, relax. You will be on the verge of taking the final step yourself in a moment. Where do you live? We will see to it that you get home safely. Do you want us to run him in? It is only necessary that you sign this statement and we can take him in right now for observation. It is up to you, lady."

One of the policemen made a tourniquet for her bleeding hand. Riding along, scouting for Jimson, they asked her to consider signing the forms, to think it over carefully, point him out the moment that she spied him. Ideal could see Jimson gliding up the street without a seeming worry on his mind, more than likely whistling that tune. She asked the officers not to bother him, let him be.

"Please let me out here. I would hate for the neighbors to see me coming home in a squad car. I will be fine now, thank you: but one thing, please tell me. Will this call go on file? I should like to request that it does. I swear if Jimson ever tries this stunt again, I will call the police, sign the complaint, visit him every day, bring him flowers, pencils, and paper. Just write this up, please, as the jilted lover, the bleeding heart. That is what they call it in the headlines, isn't it?"

"Okay, lady, just as you say. However, do not try to take the place of a good psychiatrist. You look like too nice a girl to be tied up with a fellow who will pull this kind of a trick on you. Look at yourself, at your hand. There are a whole lot of men who would be more than glad to treat you as a woman ought to be treated. Do not forget, now, if you ever need us . . . We are trained to be brave, to protect. That is what we are being paid for."

eight

△

"I have been off, Ideal, blinking at stationary stars, sieving through the dust, paddling against a maelstrom, drowning with alcoholics, rabble-rousing with students, dissenting with idealists, picketing against unfair practices, voting for the cause, walking from one end of

135

Manhattan to the other, milling around the dock in the morning shape-up, pallbearing for a kid shot in the back by a cop, imitating a caged beast that looked just like me, wiping off glass rims in syphilitic bars, rubbing out lipstick from an impersonator's welcome, vomiting up bile at the sight of a woman feeding a dog sugar with her teeth, laughing at surplus jitterbug costumes covering new arrivals' backs, ringing doorbells of old friends who have moved along, sprinkling holy water in a deserted cathedral, watching a priest lock up a silver chalice, holding down ladders for unheeded sidewalk prophets, stepping aside for stampeding crowds, watching a movie produced for the sightless, bidding for literature about to be burned, eating chili con carne with a roustabout king, dancing the cha-cha under fluorescent light, crossing my fingers at the sight of death, thinking of you who calls me not a man, tiptoeing through rich neighborhoods to not disturb the peace, floating through the park overcome by chlorophyll, straining to hear a voice tell me the reason why—the hour when, arriving in Harlem too early for grits, throwing dice until I let out an ambiguous cry, conniving with junkies to hit me again, telling long tales about women I have denied, wishing you were there to hear of my charm, walking flat-footed to ease my corn, listening to the disenchanted's story which is the same as mine, passing by panhandlers who knew I did not owe them a thing, hoping somebody would give me his courage, crying all my sightseeing down a stranger's back—a deaf-mute I turned to in a dark bar, hurrying to get home before I turned to salt.

"But why should I tell you anything, Ideal? Why should I give you visual fragments of my experiences? I can tell by the look in your eye, the twitch of your flesh, your arm's insinuating gesture, that you will reach out and beckon me to join you in bed. You sicken me, using lovemaking as an opiate. Our problems are still here when we wake up. Nothing is eased. I attempt to talk to you, to communicate everything that escapes, incenses, or moves me. I came home and told you that I quit the job, told Rheba to go advertise for another boy. And what was your reaction? Lovemaking. Ah, woman, you are not ready for me . . . Jimson quits in this moment. I quit you all. I give everything away.

"I do not want whatever it is that you are dying to give. Keep it. You are as bad as the true believers who see us as an unbending, irresistible phallus. Once we have had you, you will never go home again . . . bullshit. There has to be someone out there in the world who can sit down, or lie down if you prefer, and hear me out, listen and respond by telling me something that I do not know. My mind is made up to do nothing but contemplate that wall, intuit fully what I wrote on it. Perhaps then I will be able to finish that paper I started in school on 'The Negro as the Social Anchorite.' He is, you know . . . In spite of his allegiance and involvement, cultural contribution, influence, and transmission; coupled with infamous denials and guilt-ridden repentant ovations, he still exists as the involuntary recluse, the hermit America would rather banish to eternal oblivion.

"Political expediency, the balance of the economy, the

137

necessary conflicts without which the state would perish, supersede the social contract, the constitutional ideal, the love-thy-neighbor-as-thyself moral. Someone must be down, so that someone may be up. Obviously, my color is not the foe. Our lack of knowledge to simulate the divine force within us, that universal creative energy, keeps us always a light-year behind. Ironically, the closer we feel to duplicating the perfect image, the more smug we become. The more we tend to act the part of the Holy Father exercising mass murder in the name of righteousness, scattering civilizations to the hills in the name of peace-loving, law-abiding humanity, the closer we come to exterminating our self-created kingdom. If we would be God . . ."

"Love, you bring me full round to the beginning. Highness, I am again the low, veiled female who, un-handed by you, paused somewhere on the curve of a quiet flux. Having wrongly desired you, Jimson, I must learn how to lose gracefully what I have not found. At this moment, if I had my way, we would be somewhere where it is quiet as the center of the universe. Maybe there would be the sound of the city lending a syncopated pulse to the languid atmosphere. The atmosphere would be permeated with the musk and warmth of an exotic perfume—not too heavy, not too sweet. The scent would arouse the breath flowing through our nostrils and cause us to go on and on praising its smell, trying to define its elusive, captivating quality.

"Every object in this dream-room would bespeak a lush, sophisticated, but reverent attitude. There would be dark brown, massive, and delicate woods. Colors would be as vibrantly intense as Matisse. Some pigments would have the scintillation of Seurat, the translucency of Renoir. The light of day would be left for your arrangement. Personally, I would like a single stream of sunlight playing on the floor where minute flecks of dust and space could demonstrate their active exchange before our eyes. A vase would contain a single flower—a snow-white chrysanthemum, its center pale, pale yellow green. Some of the lone flower's petals would perk up toward the single stream of sunlight, while others would droop under the influence of the mesmerizing perfume. Others would lie at the base of the vase. We would not brush away their fallen position; rather, we would admire their accident.

"The couch in our imaginary room would be strewn with pillows of several descriptions, small, large, square, round, cylindrical, triangular. They would be plush, smooth, soft and velvet, textured roughly; so that we would touch and caress them, playing absurd finger games with the lines of their constructions. Plain pillows, Persian prints, geometric shapes, angora trimmed, tasseled. Each would conform to our bodies' contours and exude the magic of the room's splendor. Our breath would blow citrus smells down among them.

"Any music that commonly suited our equal mood would condition the room sporadically. Would either of us dare to change the stopped music? I would not feel like it myself. In a little while, I would rise to pour just one little drink or to have one little smoke of something different and strange or wild and familiar. My mouth would become rough and assertive, speaking boldly, fluently, the language of the streets. Your hair and eyes would become crazy, pitch black, bizarre as the smoke. I would be knocked out by perception. It is a gas . . . My lips would need constant wetting; my fingers would lose their nervousness that perplexes me. They agitate me so much, Jimson. Yes, I would be feeling good now. I would begin touching flesh—my flesh. I would test its receptivity. My hands would play in your wild bush of hair, with your eyebrows. My lips could not stay away from your eyes; my tongue could not stay away from your nostrils and teeth. Something would push us closer; only our knees and toes would touch. Our feet would begin prodding each other. I would toss away from you. Our voices would make sounds only lovers are able to translate.

"The spell would break itself of its own volition. Blue would filter down upon us. Sensing the change that has overtaken us, we would begin plaguing each other with questions. 'What is the matter?' 'What is wrong?' 'Do you love me?' 'Nothing,' we would answer. 'Yes, I love you,' we would tell each other, 'a little bit . . .' You would grab me harshly for saying this to you. Your body would pierce my bones. We would begin to wrestle with the blue feeling. Pressing down across our throats, we would feel its escaping. Water would run off us from every square inch of skin. You would lift me abruptly, in order to place your hand under my head. Because you have hurt me, I would frown. The flower's spiked petals are dropping one by one. The sunlight stream heats, scorches the floor. The drink belches in our bellies. Whatever it is we would be saying now, we cannot

140

hear. Our ears are being captured by the collective heart. I see the top of your head. My hands direct the shape of your hair. God, your mouth is hot, your tongue a whip. The sharpness of your teeth stings my breast. You begin to suck, mouth, chew them. Ah, Jimson, in this warm, erotic dream, you would drive me crazy, cause me to squirm against all that I desire. Regaining myself, I kiss your heart, your breast. I would kiss them as you would like, my love, never allowing them to get cold, so that the room's wind would fall upon them, coldly breaking our enchantment. The motion of our heads would begin reacting in our backs. Our senses would be directed toward our pointed beings. Our mouths would open wet, coming down fast. Teeth would bring us back into the room. Whatever you are saying again, I would not hear. We would know that it is the mood, the time of life; that is enough. Come on, now . . .

"In this same moment, I am out of it. All I know is nothing. What I would witness would make me stop breathing. Your mouth is a leech taking the blood out of me. Your teeth would clinch my spirit, while your tongue mopped my soul. My eyelids would part with tears. Everything would stiffen, yearn to cry out. Nothing would come but a groan and a dying sigh. Yes, it is feeling good as we try to procreate the absolute orgasm, the crucifixion. Death is the complete, ultimate release. We would attack each other, kiss, lick, and suck the life out of each other. Vampirically, sweat would blot up the sheets. We cannot stand it any more. I beg you to please just let me be, let me rest, find my bearings. I would plead, 'Stop this nonsense.' You would look at me as if I were a perfect stranger. My voice could not say your name. Who are you? What are you doing to me? The arrested moment would take too long. Irritated, impatient, I would feel your presence lower itself down upon me. O, God. O, my goodness . . . Ouch! Probing, it starts to plumb, push, thrust. Grunting, stammering, gasping, we swallow salty saliva. You shout that I do something, say something. What would you want me to say?

"Yes. Come on now, sweet lover, love me hurt me. Yes, it feels good. Stop! Yes, I love you. Help! Yes, you are my man. Please . . . Let me be your slave. Make me lose my mind. Let me just die. Quit! Kill me. Yes . . . Nails would plunge into your flesh. Our lips would bump into each other's. We would become our black dog, lapping it up. Wings would flutter. Snakes would hiss. Oh, we cannot help ourselves. Eyes would turn away. In the next moment, I would hear your voice lowering to make its pronouncement. My flesh would choke you, tensing for the moment. Muscles would gargle and grind, stretching toward IT. Then it would begin to ease. Your voice is distinct, each syllable rings emphatically. Our beings, extending infinitely, would come to the end of their missions as we absorb the sensation of having realized the spirit of union. The unborn world spurting tears, shooting off, would wash our old souls with a bewildering divine jangle. An angel would receive its wings. Then our beings would give us back to ourselves. Our gazes would meet to question our identities and the state which we naturally visited . . . just now."

nine

△

"Call up everybody, Ideal. Call up everybody we know, and tell them all they are invited to come and get drunk and be somebody because this is one time that a party is naturally in order."

The party would celebrate the end of the salad days; the end of living by candlelight, out of necessity, rather than choice; the finish for papering the walls with eviction notices, pretending to abhor telephones because phones dehumanize mankind and destroy the art of conversation. Stricken from Jimson and Ideal's worries would be the rationing of cigarettes in peacetime, the turning of a last shirt collar, paper linings inside worn-out shoes, one pair of raggedy undershorts and bloomers, respectively; the stuffing of a tooth's cavity with cotton, the incredible pride that goes with the last pair of flimsy trousers, a secondhand Palm Beach jacket, a pair of hand-made sandals, someone else's dress. Ideal would have to sacrifice an imported straw bag which could disguise perfectly a porterhouse steak, a roast beef custom-cut for two. Jimson would no longer have to await Ideal's good mood in order to have a haircut.

Time after time, Jimson told Ideal that "Waiting is good hunting . . ." Now she could stop hounding a savior too busy hearing his creation's plaints. Jimson had made it plain that he knew what he was talking about. In the middle of the night, a telegram startled them out of sleep. Someone had to be near death or passed away. Surely no one would be telegraphing them for money. Who among their friends had enough money to afford a wire? The manila sheet of paper fluttered in unison with Jimson's skepticism. Someone was being clever, playing a game. Ideal grabbed the trembling messiah. The single sheet enveloping them predicted, planned, and lived their future. Happy New Year was rung in by the descent of good luck, rather than an admonishing calendar measuring time. Jimson and Ideal had become so terribly accustomed to not having, to seeing blessings yearly elude them, to suspecting joy, to feeling undeserving of even the basic necessity of eating. Now that a flimsy sheet of paper was acting as emissary into the good life, they could not believe it. Having become fearful of faith, they carefully saved whatever remained within them of the inalienable rights for that glorious moment of independence and assertion, of which they knew not . . . Vaults, volitions, hope chests, and dresser drawers are crammed full of fruitless preservations designated to be utilized when the keeper has found the time to relax and enjoy life.

The telegram was faultless. It was their good day. There was a place, alas, in life conducive to the intellect and temperament of Jimson. The Bureaucratique was inviting him to join its staff of international citizens working toward the good life, the eradication of hunger, poverty, disease, the establishment of prosperity, wealth, freedom, peace, the world-wide extinction of social evils, the foundation of the homogeneous society, the abdication of caste and monopolistic dictatorship, the realization of art and religion as names for one and the same experience.

Thank you, Mr. Bureaucratique . . . Finally, Jimson's good hunting had gunned down the change from the wilderness, the way out riding astride the white dove. Quick! Jimson, salt its tail, don't let it go. Whirl it, dance it, hug it, take yourself for a soaring flight, pluck it, stuff it, gobble it up, exude its deliciousness from every pore. Go on, it's all right. There is one out there for every man.

"And let's have the party on Saturday night."

145

△

The most fastidious, methodical bourgeois could not have found one thing to criticize that Saturday night. The furniture was dusted, polished, arranged to contain a flock. Plates full of food made the table sag. Flowers and incense minimized the funk. A full moon held back the roaches waiting for the dark. The light in the toilet was working, the flush repaired. It must have been everybody's good week because every coat pocket had another bottle inside. The door kept opening for all to come on in. With each entrance came a louder sound of Miles, Bags, Monk, Bud, Diz, Rollins, Coltrane, Max, Bird, Billie, Sarah. The music's volume drowned out the crowd. Someone seated practically on top of the phonograph pleaded with the people to please shut up. Miles was playing. The song had him somewhere off on a Parisian theme.

"Up under me," the intent listener said, "I feel the walking strings of the bass and I see that black open space under the strings engulfing me, turning me into a deep tone. I am alone. You are all merely a montage."

"Oh Jesus, you're bombed," someone answered.

"Naw, he's not. The niggah's crazy, I tell you."

"Hey, Jimson, what are you puttin' down? The Bureaucratique comes looking for you, sending you a summons to come change the world."

Words whispered in some corners, begged to differ in others. One girl got carried away dancing all by herself in the middle of the floor. "Work with it, baby."

"You mean to tell me that you are voting for Adlai Stevenson?"

146

"I vote for Norman Thomas any day."

"Jews and Negroes are the only people with soul in America."

"Just a minute, I resent that; mainly because I happen to be your wife. Remember?"

"Now what were you saying about Moholy Nagy?"

"Zen? No, I am a Baptist."

"If ever Negroes wake up and fight these bastards, boycott, consolidate forces, love themselves, become willing to die for the cause, watch out! Take a lesson from the Jews."

"The only man who enlightened America was Thomas Edison."

"Hey, Ideal, you had better get Edison out of your man's pocket. So let's turn out the lights and call the law."

"Yeah, baby."

The party was going full swing. Not a soul was unoccupied, left out. Ideal ran back and forth, emptying ashtrays, keeping an eye on the few sticks of furniture for cigarette burns. Jimson, ricocheting in and out, in filtering tones of finality, sniggling down to his toes, preached his bearded wisdom of the Bodhisattva ideal. Knock. Knock.

"Somebody's at the door, Ideal." Yes, it was somebody all right . . . It was Mrs. Fitzpatrick from down at the other end of the hall. She could not help being enticed by the music, the laughter, the general peaceful disturbance. Politely, Ideal invited her to join the party. Jimson called Ideal aside demanding an explanation. Why had she admitted the old beer-drinking sop? The

147

whole building knew the old hag was crazy, hanging out her wash and patching all week long, drinking beer from Friday midnight until Sunday morning, calling the priest a son of a bitch; then being the first to arrive at Our Lady of Pompeii to sleep it off. She blessed out her poor Long Island factory-working husband like a dog, slugged and nagged her daughter from Monday through Friday, giving her a motherly word only when the girl flopped down in her obese lap her entire week's pay. The tenement-house black-cherry-lipped, dime-store-powdered, garish Lorelei, with her hair let down waist length for the ritual of Saturday night, waltzed up to Jimson, kissed him saintly on the cheek, tripped into the middle of the room, turned, posed, illuminating her spotlight with unbelievable vamp.

No need to say, Mrs. Fitzpatrick broke up the party. The room roared. Assuming that she was an unemployed actress adding foolishness to the party, one guest bid her continue and pour herself a drink. Mrs. Fitzpatrick misunderstood, and stood akimbo downing at least three quarters of a bottle of bourbon without coughing up a drop. Taking a wrinkled handkerchief theatrically from her bosom, she dabbed her lips like a hypocrite after Holy Communion. Announcing loudly that she wished the party's undivided attention, she begged pardon and bowed out to go to the toilet. The old broad should never have returned. She should have gone on down the hall, unlaced herself, taken a deep breath, and crawled into bed beside the unconscious, snoring Mr. Fitzpatrick. Instead, she returned to the party, weaving now through the partying people who had been glad to resume their individualities and balling good time. Who needed Mrs. Fitzpatrick? Enough was enough. Collectively, the guests hushed and divided themselves to allow the old girl to resume her position of cynosure. Bobbing and weaving, oozing all over herself, Mrs. Fitzpatrick called to Ideal.

"Dearie, I want to tell you something. You did not have to be so smart this evening with me. I know your kind. It is Mr. Jimson who has been kind to me. I knew him when he and the Missus first moved in here. I have been in this building all my life—born here and married here. Mr. Fitzpatrick has never made me work a day in my life. You are nothing but a cheap little home-breaker. You might not know it but since you have been down here driving Mr. Jimson crazy, taking every dime he had, he has come to me to borrow money to feed you. And now you have the coldheartedness not to want to let me in to have a good time with his friends. If he loves anyone, it's me. What have you done for him? He was going to school. He would have been somebody by now. You damned slut, you cheap tramp, I hate the sight of you, hearing you laugh, seeing him act as if he really wants you. You don't deserve such a nice boy. Come here, Jimson, Mrs. Fitzpatrick wants to tell you something sweet. I want to give you something good. I bet that you have never known a real woman. I have heard you and her at night. Who do you think keeps taking the paper out of your keyhole? Me. I had to have proof that she is the devil. I know you understand because you and I can really talk to each other—not you and that thing."

Mrs. Fitzpatrick tried to reach Jimson—she was trying,

but her legs could not think that fast. To add the final flourish to her celluloid stunt, she unknowingly trailed a piece of toilet paper, at least a yard long, from under her dress. As the crowd burst out laughing, she became more bold, assuming that it was Ideal at whom they were laughing. Theda Bara could not have slithered more admirably.

"Look now, Mrs. Fitzpatrick, I think it is time for you to go home. I have had just about enough of your nonsense and participation for one evening. I do not know if I should slap the hell out of you, pity you, or kick you out. As a lady, I ask you to leave," Ideal said.

"Don't bother her, Ideal. She is all right, a little tanked though. She does not mean any harm. Leave her alone. I can handle her," Jimson said.

"That's right, Jimson, tell her. We have something that she cannot understand. Tell her to go away. You will put me to sleep. Send the goddamned people home, too. I knew you first."

"I care less than a good goddamn how long you have known Jimson. If you don't get the hell out of here now, I will have to lose all my home-training. You are going to force me to knock the fire out of you. Leave right now, you stupid, stinking, wretched, warped witch. Have you seen yourself—toilet paper flying like a damned flag? If you don't leave this second, I will be forced to throw cold water on you—anything to bring you back, you sick bitch. Leave, please. I do not want to heave you, lay my hands on you, nor curse you. My mother taught me to respect my elders. I hope your daughter hears you down here acting the complete ass."

150

"Let it go, Ideal. I told you I could handle her. You are acting a bigger fool than she."

Most definitely, the party was over. Guests shifted, yawned, looked for their coats, stretched, shook hands, said goodnight. Thanks for an interesting evening. Ideal was not saying a word. Her adrenalin glands were working feverishly to keep up with her hard-winded nostrils and bulging veins. Her hair was uncurling, her mouth twisting into words addressed to Jimson which she was unable to utter.

"Ideal, go to the bedroom. Sit down and be quiet. You have caused enough damage. The party has dissipated. Mrs. Fitzpatrick's feelings have been hurt. I am thoroughly embarrassed. Go in the room, I say."

Without moving a single muscle or raising her voice one decibel, Ideal began calling Jimson and Mrs. Fitzpatrick everything she could think of. Calmly, she called them all names except those that were rightfully theirs. The release was getting good, becoming a Saturday night bath. Tears vacillated on the rims of her eyelids. Lord, don't you dare let her break out crying. The invalid, sleeping cap, crocheted, old Mother Good Heart had won; she had completely taken over. Cooped up down the hall, she had been drooling over Jimson, Ideal's man; consoling him, loaning him a dollar, analyzing, advising through an insight obtained from a stooped-over, sneaking keyholed perspective. Ideal wanted to grab up some heavy object in the apartment and bludgeon the two of them to death. She wanted them to die without going into a coma, fully conscious of their slayer. Did Jimson honestly believe that Ideal was at fault, wrong in her

151

assault on Mrs. Fitzpatrick? Was he so indoctrinated by his second-class vantage point that he could not help but honor and uphold white womanhood? Was he that spineless, that debilitated? Answers would not come. Nothing came but self-effacement.

Fighting off pretzel sticks, olive pits, fists, feet, teeth, hammers, forks, bottles, anything she could have put her hands on at that moment, Ideal bowed out, let the fast long-last friends have it.

It felt good to be outside, to feel cold air, to shiver and exhale the alcoholic, party-going fumes, to be able to break down and cry out loud in a tone more audible than the indistinguishable sound of silence. Ideal felt as though she should keep on walking, clicking her heels to let herself know that she was moving steadily toward the source of the night's untrackable drone. She wanted to break down, to fall apart, until her mind drained, her legs turned to strings, her memory blanked. Lying on the ground as an insignificant pile, the men would come and lead her away, strap her down in an embryonic posture, turn off the light, bolt the door, break the chain.

A dark doorway, cold as a newly chiseled epitaph, trickled down the tears. In the pitch blackness, Ideal did not see for crying; nor did she sense the presence of another using the doorway to uphold his woe. A derelict, propped against the wall, took off his hat, smiled an authentic smile beginning in his eyes and extending into space beyond his gesturing fingertips. "Ah, now, miss, there now, don't you cry." Simultaneously, mustering his stagnant elegance and affixing his feet to step one after the other, gracefully; he fumbled in his moldy vile-smelling coat and offered Ideal a cruddy ball of a handkerchief that crackled as he tried to unfold it. Not Ideal's senses, but her preconceptions of a worthless bum, a nasty, trifling tramp, were frightened toward extinction. "I am not going to harm you, miss; and I would not let anybody in this world lay a hand on you. Don't be afraid. What manner of man would I be to make you afraid?"

Acknowledging their common predicament, Ideal took the handkerchief; the derelict took her arm. The sympathetic view of herself and the thought of running into Jimson paradoxically released her last apprehension. Ideal and the derelict invited themselves to have a pitying drink.

The bar, a haven for rummies, was the last stop before the waterfront and the dirty water of the Hudson River. Not since VJ Day had the bar had such animation. Rummies and winos who had not stood up straight since falling down rose to their feet, tipped their hats, focused Ideal, commended the derelict. Ideal wondered what on earth possessed her to make her join arms with her rummy buddy and wind up in this place. The walls had not seen a bucket of paint for many moons. The chairs and tables conformed to the hung-over dimensions of panhandling souls. The place had the world's most rank smell intermingled with homemade soup, disinfectant, urine, decaying rats lodged within the walls, masters and initiates in the cult of the unwashed, peeling oilcloth, and a single woman's perfume—the proprietress.

She was an amazon of a woman, bleached blond, porcine, with huge arms like hams, porous, sweaty. She sat behind her bar peeling chipped nail polish, giving herself a manicure with her teeth. Her dress had not been changed since she inherited the business from her buried longshoreman husband. The armpits were the same color as her hair—stripped and discolored by chemicals and perspiration.

"Hey you," she growled at Ideal, "come here." Ideal knew she was no challenge for the amazon. Exhuming her dead mate might uncover quite an autopsy. As fast as she could, but trying to appear unafraid, Ideal went over to see what the big bully wanted.

"Is there some particular reason that brings you here, honey? I hope not; since I cannot supply you with anything. Don't you have a home or a man somewhere looking for you right now? You look as though you've got a pretty good nigger somewhere waiting. I don't like your looks. And further, this place is all mine, don't owe a penny. I will be damned if I will serve or sell you a thing. I don't like niggers, cannot stand them. You stink and all of your people stink."

She took a thick finger out of her mouth long enough to deliver her welcome address. Clinching Ideal's wrist, she sneered like the mother of the imperial wizard. The hand was devoid of touch and communicated nothing but a coarse, swine-natured intelligence capable of knotting a hangman's knot, chain whipping a victim already decapitated, cooking a meal for her children with the victim's still-fresh blood under her nails. The chipped polish was the color of dried blood.

Jimson preached that your intelligence will always save you. Ideal, calling upon whatever iota she had,

154

opened her eyes wider, and put on a tender innocent smile to hold down every fiber in her body itching to have its turn to insult the beast. If her cowardly feet would just be still, refuse to reveal involuntary reflex to run away, she would stand there, clinched by the wrist, hypnotizing the woman into digesting her venom and letting her leave without a scratch.

"You think you're smart, don't you? I can see what is running through your mind—if you people have one. You are not fooling me a bit. If you think that I am afraid of you or your razor, you have another think coming. All of you people carry them, don't you? I don't know if I should beat you to death for having the nerve to come in here, or call the cops and tell them you are disturbing the peace, bothering my clientele."

If he were going to live up to his word, it was high time that the derelict came forward, took away this crazy woman's vacillation. Something told Ideal to conjure up her spunk, disarm the clutching hand with spontaneous half-truths.

"Yes, you are absolutely right, you big fat monstrosity of a bitch. Sure, I think I am smart. I had nerve enough to enter your funky premises, to come up to you, listen to that shit pour out of your ignorant, clod-hopping mouth, didn't I? Yes, I have a razor; it would look good wrapped around your gizzard. Do you think that I would allow you to stand here with your filthy, stubby hand on me all this time if I were unable to protect myself? By the time that you raise up, look over the bar and down at my hand, I swear before God, heifer, you will draw back a nub. Now, I will suggest in plain English

155

that you release me, take your hand off of me. Do you understand what I am saying to you, you overgrown chinch?"

At last, the derelict found the time to get up and hold the door open for Ideal, who exited with the walkless walk of one most recently and suddenly enlightened.

The moment she was safely out that door, she would sprout wings and fly home.

ten

△

This morning I watch you from the window on your way into the first day of your new world. I see you laugh frosted greetings with the downstairs grocer. Bless him. Without him, we could have starved. I watch the half soles of your newly repaired shoes. The swing in your arm has come back. The arc it travels looks gay as you play against the passers-by. Isn't that Dosty's *The Brothers Karamazov* under your arm?

Jimson, how beautiful you are. Wonder if this employer will ask you to shave your whiskers off. I know your magic and I love you. By your step, I can already tell that I lose what I never had. And you will find me out to be a most jealous lover. Must I die in order to glorify you? Then will you believe me? I always say those things that show me less than God; although I am feeling divine this morning. Will I ever let you go? Quiescently, the most rests in not having the thing which I do not possess at all . . . Let me get up from here and kill myself. What is killing me is that I cannot give you all that you need, and I hate myself for it; but I must live to await your glory. Then I shall wish that I had left now, because I will have become some quiet sanction of your doubt, some anathema, against which you purge yourself. Oh, Jimson, I, too, wish to be liberated, although I know that in becoming your equal, we would climb over each other clawing our independent selves to death. Along the selvage of my mind, I know that we are detaching ourselves. You will tell me, "I am sorry . . ." And then I am most surely dead after a long time of dying. I so mistrust success.

I am a visitor in the land of Shinar. I am touring the Tower of Babel. Dear, dear Ideal . . . I can only sit here hung over this typewriter with my head bowed. To put down on this blankness myself freed of ego, thought, will, and senses causes my mind to empty. I am nothing. In the dream I had yesterday morning before the news came, I dreamed of a root strangling a seed. The root had my desperation. Before I went to sleep, I kept telling myself that Thursday would be IT. I am thankful. I am suspended. I cannot hit the bottom yet . . . such as, in a dream, when one is falling.

△

Awe-struck by a telepathic existence, Jimson and Ideal were united when they were separated, separated when they were united. During the telepathy's inception, Jimson used to walk into the apartment and ask Ideal what, exactly, had she been doing at such and such a time. Answering spontaneously, Ideal invariably said, "Thinking about you." In nightmares or peaceful sleep, actuality or daydreaming, they reached the plane of being able to witness their dimensional presence, gaze upon their distinct forms, hear their audible voices, feel the climate clinging to each other's hallucination. Attunement in love is a mother and a father.

This morning's telepathy was cut short. Jimson's immediate superior was coming to take him on an orientation tour of the premises. Removed from the administrative offices of the Bureaucratique, within an annex that could be reached by going either through an underground passageway or across a mall, was the office that would belong to Jimson. Personally, he preferred the isolation. As a step away from the standard green, the walls had been painted a facetious peach-blossom tint. Although the office was not situated on the somber unlit side of the building, Goethe would have been amused by the simulated peach-blossom light.

The immediate supervisor, who faintly resembled

Rheba, introduced him to the heterogeneous crew of co-workers: file clerks, typists, stenographers, translators, proofreaders, research clerks, librarians, and cataloguers. With each introduction, she provided brief biographical sketches of both Jimson and the familiar co-worker. Knowing now where the cafeteria was located, the hour for lunch, the directions to the men's room, the time to report, the hour to leave, the locker for wraps and unrelated paraphernalia, the number on the door of the supply room, the telephone's extension number, the immediate supervisor shook Jimson's hand, saying, "Glad to have you with us. If you have any questions, feel free to ask."

Jimson would have been rather pleased to know what he was supposed to do here. He knew that he had been hired and had filled out withholding-tax forms, but for what function his earnings would be taxed he had not the slightest notion. Either of three alternatives, Jimson decided, was his. He could either affirm his naïveté by questioning his function; volunteer to roll up his sleeves and pitch in to help a fellow worker, thereby working himself out of a job; or follow the predominant lead and appear efficient, bogged down by urgent business, too caught up in Bureaucratique productivity to have the time to watch the clock. It was no big thing. One of these days, somehow, he would learn just which cog he was in the wheel.

Picking up his book, he turned to his left-off page in *The Brothers Karamazov*. The first co-worker to squawk would be the office do-gooder, the brown noser, the apple polisher, the company stooge. All kinds of people passed back and forth, in and out. The Bureaucratique was a potpourri of races and nationalities, a small-scale United Nations, a sidewalk seat on the Champs Elysées. With the constant promenade, Jimson was having a hard time keeping his mind on Dostoevski. The immediate supervisor was returning accompanied by a jaunty, yellow-eyed man. Immediately upon being introduced as Jimson's departmental supervisor, the man added that he was from Barbados, West Indian; as if he were clearing up any thoughts of cultural or national identity that might have initially entered Jimson's mind. The sound of their speech was singular since American-born Jimson spoke with the more pronounced accent. The man— Johnny Lowell was his name—was splendidly dressed. His suit custom-fit him with the cocky assurance of a Beekman Place playboy. Johnny's manicured nails put the immediate supervisor's to shame. His raiment gave her the nondescript appearance of a smocked clerk. Proverbially, Johnny Lowell would teach Jimson the Bureaucratique ropes or give him the necessary rope with which to hang himself.

"Whether you are busy or not, man, always act as if you are. Never have a neat, orderly desk. Have papers everywhere. What should you care? We certainly are not on the verge of permanent peace. There would be no reason for this place, man, if there were. Day by day, you will discover that this job is a cinch, a dream. There is no one to push you; nothing is urgent. The building is air-conditioned, comfortable. The women, oh man, the women are beautiful. You can take your pick, man, any type that catches your eye—black, white, yellow, red.

161

As the name of the place implies, the institution is routine, customary, mechanical. We are specifically involved in abstract, conceptual, administrative policies. I must show you the famous file room. It is too much. There are hundreds of tons of articles, ideologies, requisitions, committee reports, projected plans, cartographic studies, resolutions, constitutional amendments, referenda, journals, agendas, bylaws, memoranda, press releases, paper, paper, paper. Talk, talk, talk. Did you fill out the papers for your company benefits, old age pension, hospital and life insurance? Come on, man, because I can talk you to death. Let's go across the street to the cocktail lounge, have a drink, see what's happening. I can tell you what your job is. No one will miss you or say a word. Remember, I am the boss. To be honest with you, man, I must admit that we are accomplishing something, but what it is I cannot put my finger on . . ."

Interrupting him, Jimson said, "You might say that you accomplish by not accomplishing, do by not doing. At once, you are the archer, the bow, the arrow, and the target. Understand. I am ready, man. Let's make it. Who is that girl?" Jimson asked. "She is beautiful."

"You don't want to have anything to do with her, man. She is the Bureaucratique nymph. Everyone knows her. Take anybody but her. Before you know it, you will know everyone here. It is the big, happy family, the closed house. We all know each other's pedigree, salaries, debts, problems, ailments, who is sleeping with who, how good a lover you are. You will become a master of chicanery at the Bureaucratique. You have the time and the freedom to develop a taste for it. By the way, your

162

job will be Second Assistant Documentarian. You know what this is all about. Remember the tons of paper I mentioned? It will be your job to figure out what they are talking about, label it, and file it alphabetically and numerically. Nothing to it. It all ends up in the stockpile anyway. You can do it with your eyes closed. What can be said that has not been said? When you are experienced, you can classify by the opening line, the last word."

A head rolled, but it was not Jimson's. If the rope would keep itself visible, lowering itself when the time came, Jimson would snatch it, attach it, and make his last grand sweep. Within these walls, he could perceive an infinite number of possibilities. If nothing else, he would have the isolation and the office machinery with which to write.

The good-luck party was a complete waste of time after all. He had been embarrassed, Mrs. Fitzpatrick hurt, Ideal dispossessed for nothing. Who was it who said he had been summoned to change the world? He would change nothing but the weight of his pockets and that would be temporary, since he owed everybody in town. He would still be working to give someone else a good meal, an overcoat, a decent pair of shoes.

For as long as he could withstand it, he would be suffocated under a deluge of carbon copies, labeling his way from down under, uncovering not one line, one word, bespeaking his liberation. Becoming another Johnny Lowell was in no way admirable to Jimson. If he were going to give eight hours a day of his life, certainly he would give the job meaningfulness. It would

163

be impossible for him to sit hour after hour listening to monotonous office gossip, lulling over far-fetched schemes for the eternal nice weekend, wondering if he would be docked for tomorrow's tardiness, paid for last night's overtime. Not one living soul occupying a desk, breaking up space in this unsung peace factory, projected a posture of buoyancy. Not one of them looked as if they entertained one thought, one supposition, relative to their intrinsic participation. Why were they here? To earn a living, of course . . . Yet they were the first to scream and protest when they were replaced by more efficient automatons. To be able to recognize the executives, call everyone by first name, know the proper department to which the buck could be passed, recognize flashing lights signaling one to pick up the phone, this collectively was the vital accomplishment, the badge of seniority. Those squatters found to be skillfully qualified to discharge mechanical duties possessed polished-brass name plates exhibiting proudly the vestige of ambition.

The complexities of organization, the created outcome, the materialization of concrete and abstract goals, were relegated to bosses, green-horned, starry-eyed idealists recently hired, bookworm intellectuals living in unreality, baggy-pants radicals classified as subversive. Talking about the boss killed just as much time. Calling him a fool for not knowing where data-processed, keypunched records were filed, resenting his issuing orders and taking two hours for lunch fueled the robots with a constant sense of worth. A common sense told them the organization would fall apart if they were not there to do the real work. Eminence can be created in robots by tightening a screw, oiling a squeak, splicing a wire, charging a cell.

None of them was going to bother Jimson. Just leave him alone, please. Stay away. He could leave them alone forever. He had not come to indulge in the absurd, hound the women, adopt the uniformed jargon and costume. The place could be the practical arrangement for getting his poems down on paper. He was sick of their giving him headaches, strangling within his throat, disintegrating into the void before he could get them down on paper. Johnny Lowell had told him that the manufactured product of the peace factory was paper. Jimson would have it made . . .

From the window Jimson looked down upon the affluent world of red carpets unrolling for men of peace, limousines disregarding pedestrians, birds being discouraged by spiked steeples, ruffled strollers being vexed by the wind, a desolate freighter forsaking the sea. A blackhaired woman passing by looked like Ideal. No, her style was not the same. Ideal wore her hair differently. Still, there was something about her suggesting Ideal. He watched her fight the wind, losing her composure. The wind, flattening against her, transformed her dress into cellophane. Jimson was further convinced that she did not resemble Ideal. He wished Ideal would suddenly appear, descending upon the Bureaucratique as fashion's trophy-lugging queen. It would be out of sight . . . She would look good dressed in gold, complementing her skin. Black sapphires, diamonds and rubies would

165

adorn her. Fur would become galvanic draped over her shoulders. He would have to buy Ideal a silk jersey dress showing off all that he knew, all that was his.

The wind, dissatisfied with its conquest, deserted the woman. Jimson watched her walk across the mall, take a seat on the private park bench, light a cigarette, open a book. He knew his senses were not leading him astray. There was something about her like Ideal.

Everyone passing under the window looked well fed, well clothed. No one reminded Jimson of himself. No one was dressed in nothing but attitude, and the simple determination not to be swallowed up by the trappings. Ideal was right. He was not persuaded by time payments, mortgages, trying to conform to some misguided standard. He was not giving his life to glamour's pace-setters, nor representing the dictates of money-hungry hucksters. Cheers! to those seeking such a shallow criterion. He had been ushered into puberty owning an automobile, dressed in elegance, being waited upon hand and foot, riding a pleasure horse cantering at his command. What was all the excitement about? Jimson would afford his aesthetic but he would purchase it through labor which he chose in right mind. Never would he go crazy selling himself for a tinsel bauble, an advertised vogue. His name, his face, his attitude, his speech, his looks, his color, were his own—different. As long as life lasted, he would keep it that way.

No need to think he would ever forget who he was, from where he came. And anybody who did not like it, who attempted to change him, could either choose to pass him on by, chalk him up as an unconvertible entity or prepare to receive the original chewing out and, if need be, a good head cracking.

The window had become foggy. The woman was leaving the park. Jimson watched her as she reversed her direction this time. The wind was behind her now. She was moving toward the annex. In a moment, she would be directly under Jimson's window. Perhaps she worked in the same building. Jimson did not know. He had decided that he did not know anything. He presumed, though, that someone else in the Bureaucratique appreciated isolation, parks, books, and leave-me-be. Still there was an indefinable characteristic about the woman that pushed his mind toward Ideal.

Jimson sat down to earn honestly his first day's wages. No one, the immediate supervisor or Johnny Lowell, had brought him any work to do. The typing paper was the most exquisite bond he had ever touched. It was as white and taut as a freshly stretched canvas, inviolate, prostrate, innocent enough to want impressions. Its watermark read Extra Strong. Jimson began a poem to Ideal, the first one from the new world:

The garden walks are too wide,
Women at their leisure welcome the flesh-hungry sun.
The memoried scents of love are not in the windsieve
    branches
Nor broken are the bushes by its form.
Through these sterile unhung walks of time
No pure passion dances
By these beams of seed-flung shade
Infinite possibility,
Your own breath's song.

167

Good God, I cry . . . Ideal would be glad to hear Jimson coming home, glad to hear whatever he had to say, glad to receive his wet-mouthed kisses, glad to blot his tears, to receive his pain, glad to say thank you for a poem.

eleven

△

While Sagittarius puts Virgo down I am superseded by imagination and desire. Stay there, understood You . . . I, here. Thank you. Anxiety shoots up everywhere this spring. For months now, through two seasons, I have watched you get up and go to your ever-loving Bureaucratique. From the corner of the window I see a spot of yellow. Spike-shaped leaves take precedent this spring. The cool ground is wrenched straining to quicken their ascension. My head is cool and harsh. You know I am sleeping late. Dreams hang in retrospect. Visions have the shapes of dog legs and bat wings; their beat is the same as a crippled man's walk. I am doing none of those things I should be doing. The sun has just come out.

Serkin plays Beethoven beautifully, softly, quickly—so much softer than the blare of our constant arguments. Is my mind moving or is it the sun? We wish so much that time will sustain us, consummate us. Jimson, since you want to be succulently involved in petals, open and display your pistils. Flower me minute flecks of yellow dust. Scent me with withering, dying smells. Stems past their green time turn to slime. Love is pruned, laughter arrested in a clipped stalk. Serkin has stopped and must be turned on again. Come, command me to flower in spite of the thorn.

Your latest poem, "Byzantine Lady Under Glass," is weighted with rainy mud. It is too down-and-out. I have been thinking on it all day long. I toy with the idea of rereading it, but who needs to induce further feelings of despair and melancholy? The woman figure is unsoluble. I keep thinking you should make it into a story. End the story on the fundamental impossibility of such a condition . . . a woman under glass. The woman must not be able to resolve herself through love—your love, if you would pattern the male figure after yourself.

My dream of love is a wild one, Jimson. My style for living an intense one—hypertense. Cool it, please, with the low-life blues. I am only able to be blue alone. Being egocentric, I relish better my pain when the pangs are confined within solitude. I like toying with it, blaming only myself, refusing to figure out solutions. When I greet the world, I cherish being together with my thoughts and problems; that is, having my mundane self in order, being independent relative to my basic needs, groomed and dressed, gas in my car, money in my pocket, absolutely free of dependence upon the world for anything other than communicative relationships, the exchange of ideas, the protests, the play. You like to hear me talk this way, yes? Have I learned your teachings well, darling?

I do not ask that you give me a damned thing. I feel guilty, uncomfortable in the knowledge of your sacrificing anything for my benefit. You do not believe that sacrifice is related or should be a test of our relationship. Sacrifice is reserved for God. The Christ complex . . . It is obvious, Jimson, that our love affair is an irrevocable trauma.

I am not joking when I say that I am deathly afraid of the responsibilities of marriage, the necessity of explanation, the lack of communication, classic, the violent arguments and disagreements, the not-having, the jealousies, the compromises, the mediations, the war. Oh, Jimson, I shake in my boots at what you call my saving myself from myself.

Sometimes I feel, through self-assertion and independence, I would be content to live alone for the rest of my wretched life. I love romance, but not constant togetherness and the multiplicity such relationships entail. The quest for man I seem only to entertain as diversion. What has happened to my faith and concept of marriage, Jimson? I have become sick, forsaken. I would rather that you have inklings of my feelings now; rather than have you leave work, come home, walk up those unending stairs, and hear the horror of my soul and black heart. Yes, I do not know in what I am interested. The previous statements are just about so much falsely oratorical bird dung. Do not let me lie to you with erratic words drenched with the sound of "I"—a housewife's meanderings. However, I know what I will not have. Lust runs out. One must be stuck, exclusively satisfied with mutual respect, love, admiration, the desire for good unto one's mate, the gift of giving one's service, compatibility; and for me, the comfortable atmosphere in which to practice and possess these restrictive, qualitative attributes.

Dear Jimson, I hope some of what I have been saying is being perceived by you—right now. Just what is it you want me to do? Telepathically, can you tell that you have trained me well? "I will teach you to become a woman, to take care of yourself." What is it that you want further of me, from me? The race track opens Monday. Yes! I want to be a winner.

The whip handle was getting hot. Come here now, Jimson. You like your flagellation from a prone position, don't you? Hurry up, get home quick now. I want to hear you beg me to whip your ass, tell me to make you bleed, to rope your back. Cringe, whimper with a putrid breath. Dare me to stop. Tell me, "Not so fast. Stay on one spot. Slowly . . ." Shed big tears about your mother, your father, Papa Boo, Catholic school, the bigoted sister, the United States Army, the Buddhistically instructive train ride on the way home from Korea, the reunion in the Apple, the snow-white suit, coming to New York, knocking on my door, Rheba-static, Bureaucratique, Johnny Lowell, the Byzantine lady under glass. I quit. I cannot beat you any more. The blood makes me sick. I am always fine until the blood comes. You ever tell anyone that you like for me to beat you? I doubt it. You tell them that your wife does not understand you. She is selfish, insane, stifling you to death, hardly lets you breathe, retards your progress, keeps you from writing verse. You ever tell them that I was on my stereotyped way when I met you, that the master had faith in her eyes watching me dance? You ever mention that I chose you instead of dance, that I wanted man, you, rather than it? You black bastard, I should kill you. I will not, though, because I will love life after having been with you. No matter why I regret and hate, I want you. It had to go down this way.

△

"It's all over, Ideal, it is over . . ."

"Yes, it's over. Hell! yes, it's over. No need to tell me a goddamn thing. I know it. I will tell you another thing, Jimson, I knew it before you did. The times we talked before we came together, you preached that business of love's not being able to last more than three years—if one is lucky. I could hear you from the beginning, but I was a vain fool. I thought I could give you something nobody else had given you. You were my answer. I hopefully thought you were mine. Conceit is a mess, isn't it? No one can have us; we do not have ourselves. You are a strangely religious man, a magnetic man, the most fascinating, disarming man I have ever known. Till the end, you are my horse. No one is more brilliant than you. Your mind is supreme. You know that I am a sucker for a smart man, and if he is beautiful to look at, too . . . Oh! my Jesus."

"Ideal, please. Those answers that you supply and ask, in the same breath, release you cleanly, completely, finally. And we play hopscotch with your green-eyed verities. It is funny, my beauty, that you think us equal in pain, but not in privilege. That which exists, exists. The madman sees that there is more. You are a fool, Ideal. Take your tears and get to your corner. Let me ram you against the wall, crush your spirit. I am a pauper, an issued man. I cannot supply you with your nature, you idiot. That is what you are really after, isn't it? You are not interested in any of those imagined states such as Godhead, grace, give and dwell. You must be aware of the weakness of man, the fixed and changing mistakes of man, the foul, the prowl, and if you do not mind, the howl, of man. No more of this please. Can you not realize that this is all so tritely psychological and that what you basically desire is a father? It is truly sad that you have missed being a daughter and torture your head with such thoughts as patriarchy. Who was it the other night that prophesied the new people? Only Edison enlightens these days . . . A bad play, but you do understand the machinization, the new light, the old order? May I feebly ask—do you? Forget it, it has nothing to do with you. Someone told me, I cannot remember who, that brute force makes the man these days, only the police are designed to protect. Those Southern boys love their mammas. Why don't you get yourself a white boy? You could snow him, handle him like a plucked parakeet. Go get Luis Pagan. He is about your speed. You did not think that I knew, yes? There is nothing to it. He is already hot in the trousers, in love with the erotic, black bugbear. You would be good as a mistress, a kept woman. You could make him let you out nights to go to nigger town. When you got back home, he would be playing sleep, twisting and turning, as if you had just awakened him from his deep sleep—the best sleep he had had for weeks . . . Well, let me tell you, the faggot would not have been sleeping a wink. He would have been lying awake, waiting for you to come home, hoping you would hop into the bed, snuggle up against him, and tell him what a boring time you had had—how glad you were to be back home. He would have a premature orgasm hearing you tell him this. Mark my words, Ideal. No matter how many killings he makes in Wall Street, blond and blue-eyed babies he makes, pedestals he constructs for blond blue-eyed mothers, he still fears the black man's joint. As quiet as it would be kept, he would give you himself, if you, a colored woman, made him believe that he was the man, the greatest piece or peace you ever had. You are such a damned fool, Ideal. Stand up, so that I can slap you down. Get up! I want to choke you to death, suffocate all that foolishness running around in your head. Let me show you what a real man can do for you. I will love you until you crawl backwards on the floor begging me to give you the most joy you can ever feel. Get up! I say. I want to turn you upside down, drive you out of your feeble mind. Let me see what you look like in the mirror. I want to strangle you to death with the sheets, smother you under my chest, pull your hair out by the roots, slap you on your butt, make you vomit telling me that I am your man. Get up, bitch! Who is your man? Call my name. Scream it. Shout it out loud. Arouse the goddamn neighbors out of their lethargy. Get up! Ideal, I want to make you pass out, lose your stupid mind. Sit in that chair. Let me watch you quiver. Hand me my belt. You heard what I said. Do it . . ."

"You really think that you have said something, don't you? Well, let me tell you something, sweet Daddy; what you have said is not what is happening. All that fancy talk does not excuse you; you are unpardoned. You understand? You are talking like a fool, a resigned one at that. What do you mean, I am the white man's nocturnal dream? What, tell me, just what do you plan to do about your own culminating dream? The first thing or next thing you think you must have to make your picture of success complete is a white girl. They tell me this is the reason our liberation moves so slowly, gradually. The white man thinks you will take over his woman and you think that he has yours. Has it ever dawned upon you that none of us is shaking such a big stick?

"Cities and bergs, divorce courts, motels, hotels, asylums, magazines, avenues, streets, districts, movies, gymnasiums, beauty parlors, cereal boxes, songs, dances, television, radio, art, minds, jails, couches, supermarkets,

176

schools, resorts, expositions, theaters, fashion houses, billboards, advertisements, want ads, jet flights, ocean voyages, overland passes, newspapers, automobiles, vegetables, meat, toothpaste, greeting cards, political candidates, mouthwash, cigarettes, laxatives, gasoline, light bulbs, religion, real estate, guided tours, life insurance, birth control, college campuses, churches, progressive educational systems, Bible schools, psychological studies on St. Theresa, St. Francis, Jesus Christ, are permeated, overrun, saturated with the three-letter word. All of us are man, woman, husband, wife, virgin, deflorated, bisexual, asexual, homosexual, the result of someone's congress. So what? It is the peacetime boom following the war of puritanism. Perhaps the nationwide excitement will eventually subside into a public practice as common as a handshake, unnoticed as breathing.

"Tell me something, as you say that I don't know. Tell me, for example, that I am crazy, that I am a freakish fool, that what I observe is auto-suggested. Tell me that you do not have a lover, that you are scheming all by your clever little self to get rid of me. Tell me that you plan to make me know that I am psychotic, just imagining things. Tell me that you do not have the courage to see yourself as a failure, that you are afraid, that you want your cake served on the silver platter, your tea rolled, your ball bounced. You jive bastard. Come on now, tell me. Try to whip me. Don't you put your hands on me.

"I have had just about enough. I am sick of hurting as only a human can, wearing dark glasses, being the sole bloody or asphyxiated body in your monthly suicide

177

shams. I have had enough of being stifled sitting in this stinking apartment, working out my penance, continuing to wash and iron your frayed shirts, your crusty undershorts; purposely playing savage with bill collectors, timing myself so that you will come home to see me scrubbing on my knees, eating moldy groceries, buying beer on credit—only to redeem the empty bottles around the corner for cigarettes, because our grocer would not let me buy them on credit—beer, yes, but cigarettes, no. I am sick of borrowing my friend's clothes to go I don't know where; but I had to make you think that I was into something, preoccupied with somebody, on the verge of breaking up our euphoria. Come on, Jimson, tell me something. You know that no matter what you say, you still have a masochist, an hysterical woman who wants you insatiably. To begin with, tell me about a Byzantine woman under glass. By this poetical image, do you mean as seen from your Bureaucratique? I am listening. Dammit, speak!"

"I do not have to tell you a damned thing. It is not I, but you who are rendered hysterical, atrophied. Don't push me into telling you of yourself. You are the personification, the effete symbol of the enduring black matriarch. You are a holdover from slavery, the privileged nonentity who was allowed free run of Miss Ann's house to dispense domestic order as you saw fit, suckle her children, give them home-training, the benefits of your orally transmitted motherwit. You were your family's provider—warm, clean, fed. Your men were devaluated, reduced to eunuchs; although some of them could have surpassed you in running Miss Ann's house.

178

It was you, however, who made the initial, lasting impression upon Mr. Man . . . humming folkloric guilt-inducing blues undertoned with forbidden sexuality. Escaping together to freedom, though, more often with you in the foreground; you and your man sneaked away concealed under your mammy-made skirts. If this did not earn us the legality of being 'freed slaves,' we commemorated eighteen sixty-three among ourselves, our patience-practicing selves, back of the big house, vowing to change our fates—now that Mr. Abe had sprouted the Union-saving halo. You sat reigning majestically, stuffed with house vittles, growing toward an obesity visually accentuating your picture of power.

"Up North, you again had the upper hand. You simply washed and starched your apron and applied for steady work; while your man, your brothers, your sons, sporadically worked. Domestic talents have never ceased to be in demand. Euphemistically, you can be named housekeeper, my woman, Mammy, any name that please you what, objectively, is nothing but a slave. In spite of cooking Miss Ann's daily meals with your bare, black hands, sticking your black titty down her sons' and daughters' throats, giving wise counsel, extricating them from feeling contemptuous of their fathers, you went further and gave away your force in the name of God's will—Jesus' name. Like any slave, you hated, despised, envied them with a vengeance. Love was worked out of you. God is love . . . You were left impotent.

"At home you played both your role and all the stock gestures and attitudes you could remember of Miss Ann's. Kicking your man around, you spit upon him for not making you a Miss Ann, taught your children to be patterns of hers. If your man were fortunate, he found work suited to a jackass; but if he were at all sensitive and intelligent, quietly rebelling and suffering from the exaggerated forces of two worlds, you beat him down, castrated him. He had to be kept down in order to keep you feeling worthy, important. Do not misunderstand me; colored men are just as proud, respectful, appreciative of their matriarchal mothers as you are. We have survived and have been recipients of their strength, sweat, love, travail. However, Ideal, that is your historic past. This is now. Are you too stupid to create your eminence in a more rational, contemporary manner? Although you are educated, intelligent, some of you black bitches cannot overcome the stamp of matriarchy. You are perceptive to recognize that it is not my fault. Why cannot you help to vindicate, uplift us?

"Bury white him, blast him, blacklist him—not us. Having grown up in the matriarchy, you desire through your emotional needs to construct a patriarchy, romantically, but never actually. You realize this is a man's world and whatever the color, woman is subjected to being man's slave. Society has constructed the law this way—not I . . . Ideal, you ever wonder why you refuse to overcome castrating a man and choose only those you are able to despise? First of all, as a woman, and secondly by being a black woman in the occidental world, you have a twofold need to assert yourself. Easily I identify with your frustrations, which are not wrong, Ideal, but human.

"Black women grow up imitating their most dynamic

daily influence—their mothers. She loved you, birthed you, understood, forgave you unconditionally, if she were endowed with maternity . . . Father was he from whom, naturally, you also wished to receive these attentions. The poor man, though, was out from sunup to sundown trying to eke out bread and shelter. When he returned, he sought distance, rest, no conflicts, affectionate but sleepy children. If he were a perceptive black man, he returned with the same wants coupled with the agonizing futility of his endeavors. Until his dying day, he would slave. Through his inhibited appraisals, he associated retardation with his family since he, too, could love only master. If he were free, responsible to himself alone, he would not take that crap for a moment. He did, though. That he did not fawn over you, rationalizing your every fault, but instead chose to set standards of hard-earned, far-reaching achievements thwarted your childish ego—sent you running to mother to gloss over those weaknesses which fatigued father objected to, corrected, and chastised. When mother berated him, denounced him for you publicly, you slept peacefully. However, it was still his mute sanction you desired to hear voiced. Can you not see it plainly, Ideal?

"Women replace unrelenting fathers with giants. You seek through him father plus all that father is not. You unwittingly chase men that reek of him; blindly you go off with them to find love, hoping that they will be, at once, giant and the father substitute. If he falls short of your superman standard, and is the same or less than father, you want to beat him to death, castrate him. To accomplish this end, you conjure up the defunct matriarch's role. The irony is that as you destroy him, you destroy yourself. You become morbidly incapacitated, imperturbable to your giant; even if he were to come calling, throwing himself upon your lap, begging you to see yourself as giantess. Aw, you fool . . . When will we let go the incestuous whirligig? I was expelled another time from school for writing as my 'What I Did for Summer Vacation' composition—a paper confessing my summer-long desire to penetrate my mother.

"Women will begin to let it go once they have found themselves, through their own efflorescence, relieved of society's family institution. Marriage is not all and everything. You need independence, liberation. Exempt from the envious tongues of fishwives and perverse-minded traditionalists who view such a woman as hetaera or pitifully undesirable, you need the freedom to live with yourself, finding reason, strength, and resourcefulness within yourself. I tell you constantly, Ideal, I will teach you to be a woman. You do not hear what I say to you. Having been enslaved, how can I wish to want you as slave? Men make women. When you are free of needing someone other than yourself to be your mind's mirror, then will you feel prepared for your giant. Until then, I am afraid that you will despise every man who cannot show you your own nature. You seek God. That is your problem. You are not a fool; you are simply lazy, self-indulgent, unwilling to reason. Leave me alone. Go off somewhere and begin to take care of yourself. We are responsible to the transcendence of selves, Ideal. Find your own way out of your self-centered restriction. I am busy finding mine. In order not to leave you without hope, completely confounded, I offer you one truth of the cryptic discipline. There is no difference between the true nature of man and woman. Our difference, Ideal, is that I think. I know why I chose you, why I flagellate you. And while we are on the subject, Ideal, let me tell you one other difference between you and me. It is neither my intention nor my need to tell you one thing about myself or my daily activities. I cannot help it if you are also in need of a father confessor. I have yet to know a woman who does not seek a man to whom she can spurt out her every blooming and decaying sentiment. Unfailingly, you are in need of a purge. No wonder man is able to enslave you or has kept you this way since time began. You give him the tool with which to work his way through your chaotic maze. Learn to tell people only what they want to hear; and that is usually more than they can bear.

"How dare you ask me to relive my life for you. I do not think in pictures, faded images, Ideal. Whatever I do is my business and don't you forget it. No, I am not falling in love nor am I seeking love. I leave philandering to the Johnny Lowells. Woman forever thinks the moment a man retires to his private needs, becomes taciturn, that he is mentally masturbating about some woman. I have not seen one yet at the Bureaucratique who excites my fingers, let alone my yoni-place. Another woman is your way out. Entertaining this figment saves you from saving yourself. I am just about sick of all the Johnny Lowells, continental shoes, continental women, manicured nails, high-styled suits, flashy cars, flashier broads. His hour-by-hour conversation is the

183

woman he is scheming to have for the night, the gin and Angostura bitters he must remember to buy, the lie he has to tell his wife. Before he can figure out the outcome of his strategy, he has spied another fox whom he will set up for tomorrow. If she is conditioned, indoctrinated into this goddamned Sodom, he will not wait until tomorrow night; instead, he will take her also along for the night. Women love him, though I cannot see why. He is stupid, vain, the Bureaucratique eunuch. They will never get me in that vise.

"You are going to keep on hounding me, exasperating me about the mysterious other woman until I begin to go for your notion. Be careful, Ideal. Truthfully, your Jimson is a poet taking time to experience whatever and whenever I can the unadulterated world of disengagement and quietude. My hurt, your hurt, the perplexing problems, remain with me, but I must take the time to be out of them, released. Please understand. By the way, from now on I have decided to be away on Tuesday nights. Have dinner with your friends or eat out. It is all right with me. I will leave you the money. I am going to study Sanskrit. Wait a minute before you start jumping down my throat asking me why. No, it will not do me any good on the job. Mainly, it gives me a discipline. The hours apart from each other will do us both a lot of good. Admit it, now; you know that we are stale. We have had it."

"Well, well, well, Jimson, you are the orator of our time. There was a time when I could have sat here absorbing each syllable, sincerely believing that you were the Messiah. Well, you are right, I am sorry to say, we

have had it. During your little speech, I could not help overhearing the hostility contained in your opinions of both black women and a world of Johnny Lowells. What about him do you resent or envy—his blissful stupidity, the charm that women find in him, his titled job at the Bureaucratique, his popularity and fashionable clothes? What is it, Jimson? You seem to know everything. What about him bugs you? Take your night out. Learn anything you like. Frankly, I do not care what you do. About your psychoanalysis of me, however, I do take exception. You miss the boat entirely. You talk about my saving myself from myself. Jimson, you should be ashamed of yourself. You have more nerve than a brass monkey. Let me tell you a thing or two, colored man.

"To begin with, you have your facts mixed up, your historical past stinks to high heaven with poolroom cynicism, barbershop interpretations, and five cents' worth of drugstore psychology. I hope to God that you are not running around the Bureaucratique expounding your black matriarch concept. People must be laughing at you as a fool. It is a fact that no matter how well one thinks he knows a person, he really does not know him at all. Never do we know exactly what it is the other person is thinking. And I sleep with you every night. Jesus!

"Now let me ask you, Do you ever stop and think about what comes out of your mouth? Do you wonder why it is that you have given the history of your people, the black people in America, such a negative, disdainful, lascivious, unintelligent depiction? The way in which you see it, Jimson, is a tragedy, a travesty. If I did not know you, I would think that you are a disguised, dues-paying member of the Ku Klux Klan. Damn! Is this what you have been learning in school? You should go immediately and get your money back. You mean what you say about being out here by yourself, the social anchorite detached from life, don't you? The last thing I ever want to do is feel sorry for you. Talking your nonsense evokes cheap sympathy. Maybe your Byzantine lady under glass possesses this sort of sympathetic response. I know, she is not real . . . merely a poem.

"It would be a pitiful sight to behold hearing you preach this doctrine from a black church's pulpit some Sunday morning, or before an audience of Masons and Grand Lodge members, before the good brothers of any fraternity. You name the group. The people would massacre you. Perhaps then I would find that real man whom I always say that I need to come and crack your head for you. Why don't you type it up, send it to any black newspaper requesting that it be published? Somebody would send the humane society after you, lock you up as a rabid dog. You say I am the fool. Jimson, I have news for you. Any literate Negro knows the historical tradition of the American Negro family is dominance by the Negro woman. An illiterate one has learned this same fact by word of mouth—oral transmission, if you prefer.

"The black woman never maintained that she enjoyed this role. For her, it was a reality, the way to survive. With the slave social system, the black man was synonymous with obscurity. It is reasonable that she would

186

be looked upon as savior, provider, protector. Although irreverent scavengers nibbled bites from her flesh, her children's flesh, too, as they lay dying raging against justice. Not every black woman enjoyed the diminutive name of Mammy. It has been said that she has never been enslaved, that in America she has always been free to express her self-assertion and independence. If the attitude toward her had been the same as the attitude toward black men, we would be proportionately as extinct as the American Indian. It is true what you say about her escaping via the underground railway. Circumstance availed itself to her; in that she enjoyed, at least, a greater mobility. She has played an undeniably strategic role in our lives. Having to rise each day and perform both her functions and Miss Ann's, practically, would instill within her a sense of self-sufficiency.

"It is her spirit, though, which you wish to disparage. Never has she, in spite of economic condition or the slave condition, allowed herself to become subjected to the male. This is what bothers you, yes? You would have her relegated to the vague, impotent position to which black men were forced to submit. You spoke of the Emancipation and celebrating, vowing to change conditions. After the Emancipation, the black woman still sustained her spirited attitude.

"Coming North in most cases proved to be no haven. It was still necessary to eat. Yes, domestic jobs are always in abundance. She took them, too, and raised many a Negro looking just like you. I hope, however, that there are not too many preaching your views. Not every man escaped concealed within her skirts, as you say. It is in-

187

teresting that you completely disregard the role which militant black men played. While they were left swinging from trees, lynched, the woman continued her 'Jesus Christ watch over, save us' determination. Again, I am thankful the militant, lion-hearted man did not share your sentiments—escaping only to save himself. You are the fool, Jimson.

"Was it unreasonable, neurotic of her to entertain visions of man, father-equaling, surpassing her dominant characteristics? These characteristics are those of independence, self-sufficiency, faith, courage, volition. They are removed from the physique, Jimson. Men are endowed equally with the same. You had better believe that we have sexual problems as a result of this matriarchal upbringing, tradition. We have become confused, transferred. Emotionally, we flagellate each other to death. Look at us . . . Experience makes me see that in America my way is less complicated than yours. Right here, in New York City, I am able to refuse three job offers to every one that you would not accept, but grab.

"Naturally, the man resents his lack of self-esteem when his woman assumes the role normally assumed by him. Living within a frustrated, suppressed, anxiety-hatched cocoon flagellates the hell out of both of them. Regarding him as a ne'er-do-well, she resents him, thinks of him as a weakling, a pimp. He, in turn, sees her as a shrew, authoritative, overbearing, a frustrated woman wanting to be a man. You are the one who brought up castration, envy of the male phallus. Really, Jimson . . . I can understand, however. It is only sensible that you must find something which you endow with a coveted

188

superiority. It would not do woman any good lying on the floor.

"Paradoxically, we are frigidly living a myth which the white man has given us. If we cannot fuse emotionally, how can we possibly yield to an act demanding abandon, communication? Certainly, we go about the mechanical gestures, but what is that? We, ourselves, seek cruelty, arguments, painful conflicts, denials as expressions of love and power. Pain is the most dynamic way to fire spent emotions. Courtship is playful combat. Because our flagellation is the result of anger and revenge rather than a conscious effort to display that pure force synonymous with virility, you will never be able to convince me that this is the erotica I dream to experience. Considering our tradition, a castrated male is the black woman's heritage. Our fathers were castrated before us . . . I started to slap your face for asking me why do black women not vindicate and uplift you. You must be blind or insane.

"I am hardly interested in dominating you, castrating you, Jimson. I am interested in your assuming the role of man empowered with the same attributes that were historically dropped in the black woman's lap. I wish to feel protected through your physical strength and intelligence. I want daily to know that you are the man in whom I have perfect confidence. We are transformed by being loved in our ugliness and imperfections.

"I realize that I have not told you anything at all. It is impossible to reach you any more—if it ever was. You wonder why I chose a man whom I can beat into the ground. I do not concede that I did. I have become so

189

desperate in my search for the giant that I allow myself to be fooled by beards. By the same token, I concede to you, who chose me, this same gross error. You, too, are in search of the giantess. We fail each other, violate each other . . . Here I go saving myself again, resigning myself to utter futility. The only thing you said of value is the way out for woman. I must find something to occupy my mind, some burning ambition. Sanskrit . . . ? You need to be studying the humanities, a living language, Marxism, socialism, history, civil disobedience, economics, political science, international relations, law, trade-unionism, physics, constitutional law—anything that will give you the stick to fight with . . .

"You plan to discipline yourself to do what—isolate yourself? Writing poetry, I would think, would be a magnificent discipline. This is nineteen hundred and now, Jimson. The myth of the self-pitying meek is being disoriented. Will its impetus catapult you into the light, or out of it?"

twelve

Δ

A kaleidoscope is defined as a device containing loose bits of colored glass and mirrors so placed that any change of position of the bits of glass is reflected in an endless variety of patterns.

A green queen ant ran up a red mast pole and fell back in a black ant's hole.

It is not true, I cry, what is said about pain. First-degree burns hurt more than birth. The design of the body is a perfection of the physical. The body is wrapped to death, unshrouded for life. It is a lack of discipline that keeps woman shrieking infinite acclamations of her holy travail. The mind, wiping away each cringe, leaves euphoria breathing out of each heaving pant. We are panted into the world in the wake of breath. We glance up at the clock to record indelibly into our minds the hour it was when the Spirit slithered out. When we think we are beholding it, we have lost it. Woman has played such a cruel joke upon man making him believe her suffering is superior. Children withstand the reality of hunger. Flowers bloom on enemy ground. Alberta slushed oil onto the fire, thinking it was kerosene rather than naphtha. The stove was on fire. The fire was on fire. Alberta was on fire, flaming, fleeing, flying past her home-cooking lunch counter out her final door. Upon the threshold were barbecued tracks.

It is not a floating God on high, contriving punishment, deciding who can withstand a dose or two. It is not a red-tail devil below, taking out ashes, proposing strategies to fix the foe. It is an ignorant woman named Ideal straining to reproduce the whole of pain, holding her breath to keep from living.

Out of accident, the chaos was borne along; so that now, evil has emerged. Evil accepts as its guise self-pity. Because of kinship, the accident that created us shatters our minds. Our souls are wrecked with an ineptitude for giving. We bear no witness of the loving heart. Compassion dwells within us on a level lower than empathy.

Why could we have not made of our ideals something constructive, taking from our experiences its creative force to bring to the world our loving attitudes? Must we make of the soil a playground for our adult temper tantrums? If our original good intention is toward ourselves, and proceeding in its normal, changing order toward mother, father, our brothers and sisters, must we employ our most evil force to gain that good intention? The intention pretends to be the act of peace.

We have a childlike concept of protection. The brat kicks and screams while shouting negative commands. Liquids ooze from his cavities; his limbs jerk in spasms. He holds his wish to be a needed desire. The willful weapon destroys his sense of play.

Studying Sanskrit is a fabrication. Jimson's taking one night out, all nights out, seven nights out, have no meaning. A Byzantine Lady Under Glass is a fragmented collection of five words streaming across this sheet of paper.

Far away . . . from what we are now is what we will become.

And I shall want to say some words of you, Jimson. Shall I speak to them of peacocks strutting their feathers, a myriad prismatic reflection of your passing me by?

△

Ideal walked into the drugstore, ordered a Coca-Cola.

A refrigerator door swung open, melting Luis Pagan into the middle of the floor. Seeing Ideal, he ran over to the corner, greeted her, and danced her around upon a swiveling stool.

Ideal was not at all pleased to see Luis, whose head

was still frozen in the shape of a cube. Trying to unthaw him, Ideal doused the remaining swallows of the Coke upon him. The drops turned into urine and spit and feces. Ringing wet with sweat, a colored boy trudged up to the counter. He must have been a kindling and coalyard worker. His workaday tool, an ax, slumped down beside him and begged for wood shavings. A cool breeze wafted into the stifling restaurant, stirring up the stench of the drenched Luis. The woodcutter caught a whiff of the smell, lifted his arm, sniffed under his shoulder to find out if it were he. Suddenly, he spied the source of the offensive odor. Spinning around, grabbing up his ax, swinging and flailing, he whacked at the ice-cube head of Luis, which chipped and flaked into synthetic snow.

"Please don't hit him. I beg you not to hit him again," pleaded Ideal. The crazed boy could not hear a word. He and Luis went dancing out the door, flaking and chipping. Chasing after them, Ideal begged them to stop, shouted to onlookers to make the boy leave the man alone. "Be careful, colored boy. Watch him. He knows judo." Two fishermen leant beside a building, cracking their sides at the ridiculous bout. Imploring them to stop the boy before Luis beat him to a pulp with a judo death hold, Ideal, clutching the fishermen's wrists, pushed them toward the center of the scene. The fishermen's scaled bellies split wide open with the laughter that had been provoked by the floundering bout. While they crumpled to keel over and die, Ideal glimpsed the color of their faces. In the night-lit panic, she had mistaken the fishermen for colored. The boy kept on settling

194

with Luis oblivious of the murderess Ideal. Realizing
that she had pushed the fishermen into dying a laughing death, Ideal flagged a streamlined train whizzing by.
The train extended its streaked motion, sneaked her on
board. The conductor unicycled through the coach singing for tickets. Ideal frantically searched through her
orderly bag finding nothing that simulated a ticket. A
stick of chewing gum was too narrow. A musty curtain
parted. A breath hissed at Ideal. Psssst . . . Laughing
girls dressed in flesh-colored steel-wool underwear sat
upon the camouflaged knees of armless soldiers. A full-
dress lieutenant issued commands, directing the laughing
girls to graft their arms upon the armless soldiers. He
commanded Ideal to produce her ticket to see the show
—or get out!

Tinkling glasses and popping corn kernels clashed
on the other side of the curtain. Ideal peeped under the
curtain. Flamenco boots and a pendulous ax rocked and
rolled in the midst of the flaky festivity. A buttered toast
was being raised to Luis and the woodcutter. They had
just joined hands in holy macaroni. Flashbulbs and
crystal microphones fizzled and broadcasted around
Ideal, quizzing her about the miraculous role of Cupid
she had played. Never in history had a snow-white ice
cube fallen for a sweaty swinging ax. Unable to withstand the bizarre merrymaking another moment, Ideal
wished herself into a grasshopper, spit tobacco juice
beyond a bubble. The act was recorded on the spot in
stereophonic sound.

The lieutenant saw what she did, ordered her immediately to change back into herself. If she refused by the

195

time he had counted to six ninths, he would order his
men to catch her and fasten her up inside a jar . . . The
jar would be labeled Insubordination. Take her away,
men. It is easy to see that she is a rabble-rouser, unable
to salute an act of truce.

△

Jimson got into bed. He nestled down from a perfumed cloud, tolling the sounds of Sanskrit lesson number one. The sweet smell, dropping down with the
sound of an avaricious guillotine, cleaved the mattress
into a foam rubber barricade. Now, Jimson, you know
better than to start telling lies . . . Just where on earth
have you been? What do you mean by that? My Sanskrit teacher is a man. Well, he certainly wears woman-
ish perfume. Goodnight and don't ever speak to me
again. I was facing reality until you came in—telling one
lie after the other.

One night, two nights, three nights . . . the lessons
were entrancing Jimson. More of this discipline he felt
he needed. He was not learning fast enough. Ideal was
learning too fast. Refusing to take Jimson's advice, see
friends, dine out, Ideal chose instead to guard her life,
watch for her dribbling man to come home—whistling
at the dawn. The fire escape was converted into a sentry
post. From up high, she could look down on lurking des-
peradoes, discover a chimney polluting the city, watch
exhibitionists peeling, direct traffic to park or continue
passing by, count the times the police circled the block,
overhear conscientious garbage men keep as much
noise as possible bouncing emptied cans against the
walls, calculate cycles by gazing at the moon.

196

When night reaches its stillest hour, unparked cars are parked, daytime activists are stretched out, all-night restaurants befriend cops with Dixie cups of coffee too hot to drink. All the moon's shenanigans have been done when Jimson comes around the corner to sweep a lunatic back to bed. The watch was timed perfectly. By the time Jimson could walk to the stoop, up the stairs, down the hall, Ideal had gathered up her cushions that rested her elbows perched upon the cement windowsill, disentangled herself from her blanket wrap—night air can be quite chilling—jumped into bed, and slept—dead to the world.

Clanking down, accidentally hitting the guillotine barricade, Jimson dozed off to sleep, relieved that Ideal was growing accustomed to the schedules of a discipline-minded man.

Stealthily peeling back the blankets, holding her breath, slipping out of bed, afraid to death she would awaken the man, Ideal, the sentry guard, tiptoed to the closet, gathered up the sleeping man's uniform, tiptoed upon those floorboards which were solidly nailed, closed the squeaking door, silently daring it to make a sound. Switching on the bright lights, Ideal began tearing through Jimson's pockets, dashing out unaccountable coins, holding up his shirt to the light, frisking down his underwear, unfolding his handkerchief, upturning his foreign-soiled shoes, sniffing his tie, inspecting each article like an examining coroner. The devil comes to the aid of nutty women and witches. Ideal never could decide what she would do if Jimson would get up to get a drink of water, go to the toilet, come to see what she was doing. He was always exhausted after the lessons—thanks to detumescence. As surreptitiously as the clothes had been brought into the light, they were returned—each article replaced exactly as it had been originally hung. The next item for inspection was the waft of perfume. Did Jimson's emanation coincide with that of the clothes? Being satisfied with her ability to enact the methodical inspector, Ideal retired to the living room to riffle through his portfolio, snoop through his poems, decipher their covetous, lustful messages. Cigarette after cigarette filled up the ashtray while Ideal read through the poems, breaking her own heart by finding meaning even in the words *but, and, or.*

Jimson had informed Ideal time after time that she was a complete fool, incapable of thought, anxious to save herself by unreasonable means. Ideal could hardly wait for morning and inquisition time. Badgering Jimson while he shaved, took a bath, drank his coffee, brought not one hint from his lips affirming Ideal's nightly findings.

"Ideal, you are imagining things. That is not lipstick. I use a red pencil on the job. The ink gets on my hands. I have the right to write anything I please, if you do not mind. There is hardly a soap on the market that is not perfumed, you idiot. Darling, you have got to get some sleep, some distance, something to occupy your mind. You will drive yourself mad trying to keep up with my plans. You are really losing your mind, woman. Take care now . . ."

Ideal screaming and ranting, calling Jimson a liar, yanking his tie, tore at his shirt, threw his hat and

198

all those mornings that you jumped up cursing me out for having to go to work, calling me the vilest names you could say, talking about my upbringing, my mother. You used to loan me a dollar as if I were the most despicable object you have ever seen. Remember those damned castanets? You used to lie in bed clicking them until I thought I would go out of my mind. That is red pencil, Ideal, common household soap, those strands of hair are yours; mine certainly is not that long. Go to sleep, will you? Damn!"

Deciding that he simply had to sleep nights, if he were going to keep his job, arrive on time, and enforce purposeful disciplined punishment, Jimson gathered up his pillow and blanket to get some sleep in the living room. It did no good.

"I have been giving our situation a lot of thought, Ideal. This evening I am bringing one of the fellows from work home with me. I have asked him to take you out. He is crazy about dancing and balling it up and down all over New York. I think that it will do you good. Gives you a chance to get back into the world. I don't know why you have given it up. Yes, I know that you are raggedy as a can of kraut; but one of your girl friends will be glad to lend you something to wear. They all hate me anyway. It will enhance their hatred and their good-samaritan inclinations. Will you? You will like him. He is a nice fellow, harmless. You do not think I would send you out with a monster, do you?"

△

An introduction to a rapist is a courteous, affable event. He smiles, stands tall, shakes hands, calls you by

name, and does not dance on your suede toes . . .
Giving Jimson a reassuring, healthy handshake, smiling
his widest toothpasty grin, the rapist told Jimson, "Don't
worry, man. She will be fine with me. I will get her back
safe and on time." Jimson wished them the good time
and inhaled relief. It was just fine with Ideal, too. She
had her definite little scheme in mind. Before the night
was over, old hickory nut head was going to tell her
exactly what was going on at the dear old Bureaucratique. Well, all right, let's go dancing . . .

In the middle of Manhattan, there is a place called
the Gay White Way. The street vivisecting the Way
straight down the middle is called Broadway. The name
puckers on the lips of newly arrived challengers, gushes
into frostbitten Oooooo's blowing out the mouths of off-
season tourists, spits out as slang by "up the street" cats,
gargles in the larynx of Greenwich Villagers viewing
it as a side show, hesitates to be dignified by world-
traveled snobs. The bedazzling milk-white lights that
gave the shimmering strip its name have been seconded
by gaseous tubes advertising and aerating a congestion
of impure colors. Looking up the Way from Forty-sec-
ond Street and Times Square gave Ideal the blinded
impression of initially looking up the passageway at the
Crystal Palace. Tonight, Ideal felt as if she were a bit
of colored glass on the verge of being recast into an
asymmetrical salt crystal. The rapist, still smiling broadly,
reached into the car's glove compartment and pulled out
opaque glasses. Abracadabra . . . an Abyssinian prince
home from a mission. This should make you laugh,
Ideal, take some of that dejection out of your spine.

202

They had picked the perfect night, the legendary night to go to the Palladium—Wednesday night. You could cut through the smoke and steam with a butter knife. Footloose people from every walk of life dance on the sidewalk below the place, up the stairway leading to the ballroom, at the cloakroom window, past the ticket-taker's stand. It is wild, infectious.

Colored lights and mirrored chandeliers revolving in the ceiling cast sparkles and diamonds and oblong hearts. Mankind just changed to polka dot. Simultaneously, two bands of huffing, puffing musicians blow, beat, and finger rhythms and beats which make the dead rise up to cha-cha one more time! Arriba! Abruptly, during an uncompleted crescendo, the musicians stop to take a breath. A human herd stampedes to the bar which is a multitude of feet long and as wet as the musicians who played the joke. Spilled Scotch, V.O., bourbon, rye, gin, rum, beer, wine, and soda, flowing together, forms an efficient alcoholic stream to swim the sliding, spinning shot glasses into the hands of a first-come-first-served abandoned crowd. Before your booze is up to your lips, the music starts up again. Show time! *Un poquito de tu amor—un poquito nada más* . . . Yes, the Abyssinian prince danced beautifully. He was too busy mamboing now to ask him a few pointed questions.

"Let's get out of here. You like belly dancer joints?" "Yes, but will arak mix well with Scotch?" "What does it matter? You don't live but once. Let's split."

An endless string of kohl-eyed girls, beer-drinking mammas, dime-store-wigged floozies, walked in and out of the ladies room. They disappeared on the other side of

203

the door dressed in civilian clothes. When they reappeared, they were transformed into hootchie-kootchie, Queen of the Nile, Sheba, Cleopatra, Little Egypt, Samia Gamal, the daughters of Thoth, the sisters of Bubastis.

"But, tell me, aren't they all wearing the same costume?"

"Well, hell yes! Who did you expect—Princess Yasmina? You want to try a stinger? Jimson drinks them all the time." At last, the smile was coming to the point.

Fishing around, throwing bait, dropping hints, trying to keep up with the waiter who was serving them mighty fast, was proving to be the umpteenth wrongdoing of Ideal's life. Entranced, she spiraled out to the center of the floor, and started to roll her belly in involuted twirls. The daughter of Bubastis leapt from the stage, arrested Ideal, tossed her veil demanding that they go to war. The dancer did not know that a little night war was right up Ideal's alley—second nature. The manager, mentally converting into dollars the number of hands waving the waiters to hurry, beckoned the oud player to keep on strumming. The clamoring spectators whoopeed! Maybe he would add the bit to the act . . .

"You have had enough, Ideal. Come, girl, let's get out of here. Jimson would never forgive me. I could never live it down."

"Leave me alone. I am fine, I tell you. I'll kick this broad's ass from one end of this bar to the other. If you want to do something for me, tell me what's happening at the Cureaubratique. Aw, hell . . . you know what I am trying to say."

204

The conniving sneak. Those were the kindest words he had heard all evening. The drinks clobbered Ideal into a diaphanous veil. She did not care where he took her; so long as he took her out into the air, please. The prince whisked up Ideal, galloped out of the bar, jumped into his car, locked the veil's door to keep her from flowing out, stepped on the gas, and went racing out of storyland in search of an actual castle.

"Just a minute. Wait! Stop this car. Turn around. You went past my street. Where are you taking me? Brooklyn? I don't know anything about Brooklyn. Went there once to visit a sweet girl who had just had a baby. Take me home, I say. I want to go home now!"

"Be quiet, woman. I am going to take you home, but first we are going to my place. You have to be sobered up before I can take you home to Jimson. He would have a fit. Stop it. You are acting like a little girl. No one is going to bother you. Just relax, please . . . ."

Zooming through Manhattan on the way to Brooklyn with a stomach full of cha-cha, Scotch, arak, stingers, and an indigestible daughter of Bubastis is equal to a medically administered lungful of cyclopropane gas. The prince was saying something now about take off your shoes, relax. "I'll switch off the light so it won't bother your eyes. Rest."

"Rest? Take off my shoes? I don't want to rest. I want to go home. I don't drink coffee out of my shoes. God-dammit! where am I?" The hooded prince was transmuted into a maniacal beast, shoving and pushing, prodding and feeling. Damn! he was on the brink of breaking her neck trying to force her head on the pillow for her relaxed benefit. His old hard knees bruised her shins, prickly whiskers scratched against her face. His breath smelled worse than hers. Tussling and warding off a determined, panting, hard-breathing, long-legged, frantic, dog-natured drunken man is such a pathetic, absurd, complete waste of time. "You ought to be ashamed of yourself. If you have to fight and scuffle with a drunk woman to get yourself a little bit, well then, Mister, you obviously are not qualifying as a man. Don't you like conscious submission, you inadept rapist? You had better get up from here and take me home. No, on second thought, lie down here and let me give you an example. No good, sweet lips . . . You are definitely not what is happening."

Nothing Ideal was saying was making any sense to her; but, soothingly, it worked upon a neophyte rapist. His hope was restored. Maybe, if he would act nice next time . . .

During that vertiginous, head-shattering, sinking, safe-at-last moment which blacks out a binge, Jimson stalked into the room, distracted the whirlpool.

"Doggone you, I will kill you if you say one word!"

Jimson, detonating Ideal up out of her heap, demanded to know what she had most recently given away. She could not convince him, considering her torn-to-pieces-looking sight, that she had gone out and conducted herself as a well brought up Filipina, a married woman . . .

"No, nothing you say will change my mind, Ideal. You have torn your drawers this morning. Here I am thinking that I am doing something kind for you, sending you out with one of my friends to have a pleasant evening. And what do you do? You go out and act like a slut, ruin my reputation, come home in broad daylight looking as if you have been off to the moon and back. I will never forgive you for this, Ideal. Now I am most definitely out. Don't you forget it. Mark my words, you cheap tramp. You are to blame. You have diminished my respect for you. Whatever happens to us is your fault exclusively . . ."

"Look, Jimson, at this point in life, I cannot hear a word you are saying. Please save it until later. If I don't lie down and get some sleep, I will either die right here before your eyes by vomiting myself to death, attacking my heart with my own bare hands, or choke myself to death to keep from hearing that two-faced, fake crap coming out of your offended-sounding mouth. Go away, please . . . I am sick, you cheap charlatan."

Ideal knew how to scheme about as well as a fly trying to eat the sweetening off flypaper without being stuck. Making up her mind that it was revenge, a slice of the smiling one's prepuce that she wanted, Ideal wrapped a bayonet, a war souvenir of Jimson's, within a silk gauze scarf. As she stepped into a cab to go to the Bureaucratique and publicly stab Smiley to death, Ideal thought twice, changed her plan. She would call him and tell him that she could not get him off her mind, that she wanted to give up a bit. Flattery will get you somewhere . . .

Telling her that he would meet her within an hour, he arrived within ten minutes. She wanted to go for a ride, hear all about him. Where did he learn to dance so well . . . The conversation and ride would suit him just fine. During the conversation and bragging about his sensual prowess, he inadvertently slipped, spilling out exactly what Ideal needed to know about the errant Jimson. Calling the ride quits, she asked the romance-spouting driver to take her back home—she had forgotten something.

"Anything you say, Madame. Name it, but where shall we go after . . . ?"

A sharp curve in the road threw her bag with the silk-covered bayonet onto the seat. Reacting as the perfect gentleman, the smile reached to upright the bag. The scarf had shifted. The blade, pointing dead between his eyes, cut the engine off, excised his tirade. He was surprised, betrayed, duped, enangered, tricked, insulted, and crazy enough to stab Ideal to death for trying to be so smart.

"Let me take you home, woman, before I do something I will regret. You are not worth it. Well, I can see why Jimson is running around. You are enough to drive the poor man out of his mind. Don't you ever think to try this trick again with anyone. Someone will make you eat that thing and beg for the handle. And, on top of it all, you have caused Jimson to become angry with me . . . telling him that I tried to rape you, running home as if you were innocent. Are you serious? Your own husband does not want you; so what makes you think I do? Nobody wants you. You are a sick woman. Let me take you home right now."

Feeling like the last grand blundering idiot, in addition to being a cuckold, Ideal got out the car, slamming the door with such a bang that bits of brick dropped down upon her dog-tired head. She stopped at the grocer's to buy out his ale—on credit. In order to buy cigarettes, she needed six bottles' worth. She took the bottles upstairs, poured their contents into pots and pans, looked from her sentry window to see if the grocer was standing out front, walked back downstairs in the other direction to avoid having the grocer see her lugging off his bottles.

The Byzantine lady must have had other plans this evening. Jimson came home early. No, she had no other plans. From the look on his face, he had argued with someone disallowing him the last word. "I am sick, Ideal, just plain sick of the whole goddamn lot of them. The entire Bureaucratique can pack up and take a chartered bus to hell for all I care—every damned one of them: the shaded ones, the gray ones, the striped ones, the plaid ones—all of them. I have not met yet, on the face of this earth, a soul ranging in color from ebony to albino who does not have the entrenched opinion of thinking himself to be superior to a Negro. Girl, we really have a hard way to go and a short time to go it in.

"I was sitting at my desk minding my business—and who should come along, but your dear old friend Smiley, dying to tell me about his newest conquest. All of a sudden, my door flew open presenting a funny-looking blond girl. I had never seen her before in my life. Behind her was the chief supervisor. 'Is that the one?' She pointed in my direction; although with a person with light-colored eyes, it can be rather difficult to tell exactly where their vision is focused. You know what I mean?

Well, anyway, she hesitated, stammered, and then had the antediluvian audacity to utter, 'It is hard to say. They all look just alike.' Now you know that Smiley and I resemble each other about as much as an anteater and a glowworm. Coming closer, practically down my throat, squinting to see better, she pointed her finger at Smiley. It seems that he took her out for a few drinks and ended up in Brooklyn. I doubt that she will get away with prosecuting him, although she wants to. She gave me the impression of possessing quite a smeared subconscious herself. This is not the first of his offenses. I must admit that I knew about him when I allowed you to go out with him. I did not think he went for colored girls, although he is blacker than I am . . . To add the final blow to the story, I mentioned to uh . . . , well, I mentioned the scene to one of the women to whom I can speak in the place. Immediately, she defended the white girl and ended by calling me all out of my name. It is a hopeless situation. The second that you begin to believe that people are people, old Jim Crow comes buck dancing between you, laughing his head off like an outdated minstrel who has not been advised his day is over, or that defamation can be prosecuted."

"Jimson, I wish to add just one single grain of salt to your bleeding heart. I do not feel for you—not one bit. Answer me this, please. When you were being stoned by your listening ear, did my incident with your rapist cross your mind for maybe one minute? I hardly think so, my friend. What do you mean—you did not think he goes for colored girls? Jimson, you knew when you

210

brought that well-dressed pervert into this house what
could probably happen. And you more than likely
planned it all; in order to give yourself a legitimate reason for washing away your egomaniacal piggishness. Do
not say another word to me about anything, please. It is
singular that you choose to come home and cry the
blues to me about your phantom confidante. I thought
she was so understanding . . . Shed your self-imposed
tears on her chest. It probably has blue hair. I don't care
to hear it. Well, this beats all I have ever heard. Jimson,
you are too much. I cannot get over it. I do not know if
I should laugh, cry, cut your throat, jump out the window, thank the Smile for lifting the veil—or what. It is
just too much. I cannot get over it. Jimson, you are
something else. Really! Well, Jesus! and he sent me out
to be raped. Are you ready?"

"No matter what you may think, Ideal, there is no
other woman. I love you. I know, and every day it is
proved to me, more and more, that you are my woman.
Okay?"

"Jimson, shut up! Go to bed. My day has been just
as chaotic, just as revealing. Hell no! I do not want you
to sleep with me. Stay out there on your ascetic couch.
All those nights in which I begged you to touch me,
cried and sniveled all over myself, pleaded, crawled,
whimpering for your love—shit! I must be crazy. Stay out
there. Contemplate your discipline. And that 'now you
are to blame' bit. Well, Sakyamuni, as I live and breathe
. . . and I was fool enough to fall for it. You are absolutely right, Jimson. I must be a bigger fool than I know.
Your one true friend puts you down—so here you come

looking for me. Now, this is what I call a real bitch, a natural bitch, a nonsynthetic bitch. You are too far out for me. Let me get out of here before I try my best to kill you, to take you out of your misery, you black stinking dog. Yes, I said it. Just what do you plan to do about it? Run to your Byzantine lady? Tell her your secret, undisclosed wife agrees with her and calls you a black dog to prove it. This time I request that you go. Go on, run to her. And, on your way, imagine how you would like your flagellation this time. Name your instrument. Name it, so that I can whip your behind until we eradicate the world of hurt. Think about it. You have the time. I can wait forever."

"There is no woman under glass, or under anything else, Ideal."

"Aren't you tired of that lie, Jimson? You deceive yourself, her, me. Why can't you stand up and become a man? Why wallow and die trying to secure illusions? You castrate yourself gaping at advantages denied you; and flinch and turn your back upon the one accumulation that would make a man, an eclipse, out of you. You know which advantage this is, Jimson? It is the empowered volition to make your own choice, to choose your own way independently. No one gets out of the world alive . . . Denounce the slave-nature, the reactionary stigma. Who is enslaving you? Wring the predilection out of them. You sicken me walking around spouting your death-wish doctrine. That went out with Tristan. You uphold the patriot who believes that you are only happy being enslaved; since, after all, it was God who created you 'different.' Transmute the terror.

Change your mythical virility into courage, your commendable knowledge into spirit; disavow your history of being the mangy, flea-bitten, unvalued, black underdog. Go on out there. Sick yourself on them. You will be stimulated seeing how the cowards fall back behind their bed-linen curtain. Tell them plainly that you will not accept another depravity. 'I Am hath sent me unto you.' Give them the hope that you will retaliate with an equal persecution and annihilation. Sit down on them, strike them. If I were a man, Jimson, I would give you the beating that you desire. This is your thrill, your kick. You would like a man to beat you down, especially a white one. The idea is fixed in your mind that you deserve it. You have come to expect it, anticipate it. Once, so violated, you will feel delivered, free of the calling of your manhood. Beatify yourself. Imitate the life of your favorite martyr until it becomes your life. You are going to die anyway; so why not die for the black dog, for the Sanskrit-disciplined poet, the Byzantine lady, Smiley, the daughters you will have created. Men make women . . . yes, Jimson?"

"Yes, Ideal. And some women accept me just as I am. They don't try to make me over, play the matriarch. They encourage me, answer 'Yes' to everything. It is easier that way . . . One of these days, all you colored women will wake up to this fact; then you will keep your men. I am sorry, Ideal, but you know that men are weaker than women. When you saw me becoming less than I really am, why did you not stop me, lock me up, take me by the hand and lead me away? You know I love you. I would have come back home. I just asked

213

for you to wait for me . . . that's all. And now that I have caused you suffering equal to mine, and you still love me, I want you, Ideal."

"Jimson, Jimson . . . you are my own true love, but I cannot take it any more. Just go out there and find your giant, kill him, become his spirit. Please just go away now, I cry. Let me be alone. And, Jimson, please remember to close the door."

Δ

Paris
13 February 1966

coat onto the floor, stomping upon them, dashed half-finished cups of coffee in his face. "That ought to do it. Now you will be late for work. And you know, you raggedy bastard, that is the only shirt you have."

An hysterical woman is a bitch without a peer . . . Jimson abstained from moving a muscle, lifting a hand. Quietly, he gathered his clothes off the floor, dabbed the steaming coffee off his beard, concealed the ripped shirt as best he could. "I will be home early this evening, Ideal. You need me. I want to talk to you."

"Don't do me any favors. I don't need you. Go to your woman under glass. She needs your prevaricating tail, not I. It would please me if you never come back. I hate you."

Talking to Ideal served no purpose other than stimulating them into pummeling the reconciliation out of each other. There was no way in life for Jimson to convince her that he was innocent. She had never come across one single sheet of paper containing one word of Sanskrit.

Through standing guard as a fire-escape sentry, playing inspector while Jimson slept, Ideal mastered the science of cryptograms, developed fully her olfactory sense. Ideal, at last, had found her burning ambition, that thing which she sought to occupy her mind. What was this? A new clue had turned up . . . a blue hair. Thank Con Ed for bright lights. Entangled in the lapel of a Harris tweed jacket, Ideal detected a minute strand of blue-black hair. So Miss Byzantine dyed her hair, the old broad . . . She put it between the pages of a book in order to verify her findings in the morning sun. Ideal took pride in being heliocentric. Her conclusions were right. Nightly, blue hair was put between the pages of her judgment book.

Jimson stared with mouth-hanging amazement at the wild woman whom he had vowed to love and protect forever. It became impossible for Ideal to look at Jimson without going into a rage. The clues began producing themselves with such a furious nighttime regularity, Ideal could no longer contain her attacks until morning came. Jumping astride the bedded-down Jimson, flashing on the light in his sleeping eyes, cussing and riveting him down into the pillow, hoping to suffocate him, Ideal pleaded with him to ease her mind. She knew that she was not crazy. Hair is hair. Lipstick is lipstick. Perfume is perfume.

"Jimson, all I ask is that you please tell me that it is not my imagination. I would be a fool to keep you from doing what you wish. It breaks my heart, though, for you to deny it and try to make me think I am being consumed by suspicion. I do not ask you for names and details; I merely want to be relieved of this stupid self-infliction. I cannot understand why you keep denying every strand of evidence I stick under your nose. Why must you continue to lie? Can you not be a man once in your life and say, 'Yes, Ideal. So what?' I know that you have left me. Tell me, Jimson. It is too much. I cannot take it."

"Ideal, I have had just about enough of this. You will drive me crazy with it. I told you a long time ago that I would flagellate your mind—not your body. You are simply feeling the degree of pain which you caused me

CARLENE HATCHER POLITE *was born in Detroit, Michigan. She studied with Martha Graham in New York and was subsequently invited to join the original Alvin Ailey Company. A former member of Actors' Equity, she has had experience as an actress and theater manager. In the sixties, Ms. Polite returned to Michigan, served as assistant to Coleman Young, was elected to the Democratic State Central Committee, and was coordinator for the Detroit Council for Human Rights. From 1964 to 1971 she lived in Paris, where her first novel,* The Flagellants *was published; American, British, Italian, and Dutch editions followed. Her second novel,* Sister X and the Victims of Foul Play, *was published in 1975. Ms. Polite has two daughters and now lives in Buffalo, where she is a teacher of Hatha Yoga and a devoted student of Yogi Raj Bua Swami. She is an associate professor of English at the State University of New York in Buffalo, where she teaches creative writing and Afro-American literature.*